F
BUR

Burchardt, Bill.

The lighthorsemen

DATE		
Withdrawn		
WMQTN DAT		

2-19-04

W 5-15-93
W 12-31-03
W 12-18-06

DATE DUE
03/20/06

THE LIGHTHORSEMEN

Also by Bill Burchardt

SHOTGUN BOTTOM
YANKEE LONGSTRAW
THE BIRTH OF LOGAN STATION
THE MEXICAN
BUCK
MEDICINE MAN

THE
LIGHTHORSEMEN

BILL BURCHARDT

DOUBLEDAY & COMPANY, INC.
GARDEN CITY, NEW YORK
1981

ISBN: 0-385-17148-X
Library of Congress Catalog Card Number 80-1986
Copyright © 1981 by Bill Burchardt
Printed in the United States of America
First Edition

PREFACE

In the Indian Territory, the Lighthorsemen maintained order in the Cherokee, Creek, Choctaw, Chickasaw, and Seminole Nations. Few in number, virtually unequipped (each purchased his own horse and firearms), these policemen, themselves Indians, kept order in an area larger than five New England states combined. This novel imagines a task force of one from each of the so-called Five Civilized Tribes, assigned to the Union Agent at Muskogee. It attempts to picture with verisimilitude that colorful time and place, and the personalities of typical men who served as Lighthorsemen.

Indian justice was summary and promptly administered. There was constant conflict between the federal courts and the Indian courts. It was a hard time, during which tribal unities were diluted by the pressure of colonization by white settlers. Groups do not always survive, but certain heroic individuals do, often with a zest and cheerful spirit that makes the intolerable tolerable.

Bill Burchardt

THE LIGHTHORSEMEN

CHAPTER 1

Two of the Indians were chopping down a telegraph pole.

The third lay resting on a nearby hillock. He watched them good-humoredly. The three Indian policemen, each in partial uniform, evidenced the "betterment" of acculturation and showed some acceptance of the white man's ways. If their activity was renegade, putting them in a position of danger, they showed no apprehension of it. The foreheads of the two choppers were beaded with sweat, but the third appeared fully at ease and relaxed. They seemed clear of conscience and evinced no guilt.

Young Johnson Lott, swinging a double-bitted axe, wore blue uniform-issue britches thrust into high-topped plain black boots. His loose-knit butternut shirt had been decorated with bright-hued ribbons which streamed down his back from his shoulder seams and from beneath his breast pockets. From the band of his uncreased black sombrero, a turkey feather with beaded quill swept back like a weathercock. He was clearly pure-blooded Muskogean Creek.

Seminole Mutt Kiley's garb was reminiscent of his people. A casually wound turban gracefully adorned his head. His powerful arms swung a single-bitted axe of work-polished, silver-bright metal. His Lighthorse jacket of blue, faded white in spots, swung open in casual ease over hard-woven ducking pants and worn leather work moccasins. Except for the jacket, the earth tones of his garments blended indistinguishably into the landscape. Even the turban, with its interwound layers of brown and green, did not seem exotic or out of place against the grass greens and tree-trunk browns of the rolling land.

Captain Millar Stone, Cherokee, wore a coonskin cap, fringed buckskin shirt, leather breeches, and government-issue brogans. Resting supinely on the hillock, he seemed as common as the ground on which he lay. Staring up at the heaped white cumulus clouds that idled westward in the blue April sky, he poked a jibe at the young Creek warrior, gently, pleasantly. "Keep up the beat there, Private Lott."

"Yes, sir." Johnson Lott seemed imperturbable, noncommittal, intent on his work.

The Seminole Lighthorseman stopped chopping and leaned on his axe.

Like the sound of a wheel suddenly gone flat, rolling around its rim to land jarringly on the flattened iron, Johnson Lott's axe stroke went on, its rhythm broken by the emptiness of silence where Mutt Kiley's axe had formerly struck the pole.

"What's your problem, sergeant?" Captain Stone scrutinized the Seminole *micco* with twinkling eyes.

"I've figured out that it's your turn," Mutt Kiley responded as he gazed off over the rolling, timbered hills. A broad timber cut stretched back eastward across the hills. At intervals along it lay the telegraph poles already chopped down, each fallen pole entangled with severed wires. Ranging southwestward, the timber cut continued with newly erected telegraph poles still standing, the naked newness of their crosstrees glistening with strung copper wire.

Millar Stone, resting his head on the hand of one cocked-up arm, said, "Sergeants and privates do the heavy work. I just supervise." He moved to lie down again, but something seemed to catch his attention and he sat up, lifting his nose to smell the air as if he were trying to identify some vague, illusory odor. "Wait, Johnson," he said.

The young Creek Lighthorseman stopped chopping. He stood silently, lifting his head toward the east as he, too, sniffed, testing the air.

"Sweaty horses coming," he said with certitude.

A long minute passed before a faintly distant harness jingle confirmed his prediction. Millar Stone stood up. Lott and Kiley were standing with their axe heads resting beside their footgear, the round-shouldered, chunkier Millar Stone slightly behind them.

Stone reached to touch their shoulders, dispersing them, and Lott and Kiley, leaving their axes, moved away until the three of them stood widely apart in a semicircle, some thirty yards separating them. Each had a steady hand hung in close proximity to his sidearm.

They waited patiently. The sounds of the approaching vehicle increased as it hove into sight over the far ridge. It careened toward them along the line of chopped-down poles. On its front seat rode two telegraph company troubleshooters. One drove; the other held elevated across his chest a double-barreled, sawed-off shotgun.

The wagon was loaded with repair paraphernalia. As it came closer, coils of rope became visible, flapping loosely along its sides. The wagon carried shovels, sharpshooter spades, a pair of pickaxes, spools of wire, climbing gear—all the equipment necessary to repair a break in the telegraph line. Along the sides of the dark green wagon a painted lightning bolt embraced the legend WEST UNITED TELEGRAPH COMPANY.

Each tool and piece of equipment was neatly strapped into place in the flat wagon bed, but the rope coils flapped wildly as the driver tugged and sawed on the reins, swinging the vehicle broadside as he pulled to a halt. His partner was on his feet, his knuckles white as they tightly gripped the stock and trigger of the shotgun.

"You'll put back every pole you've chopped down!" he shouted, and swung the shotgun in a slowly threatening arc.

The three Indian policemen stood silently.

"Don't any of you speak English?" demanded the bloodless-knuckled shotgun wielder.

"Well enough," Millar Stone said laconically.

The wagon team jostled muscularly in the harness and the

driver bellowed "Whoa!" as he heaved on the tight interlacing of reins in his fingers. The shotgun man staggered, but he did not fall.

"Speak up now!" he demanded.

"About what?" Stone asked blandly.

"About these downed telegraph poles!" The irate inquisitor spread his legs farther apart for a better purchase on the wagon bed. It made an unsteady platform as the nervous team still shifted and moved restlessly against the whiffletrees.

"White man," Stone said firmly, "you have no permit to put these wires across Creek Indian country. Ol' Sam Tsch-kote has been agitating the Union Agent to stop you."

"You let the Katy cross all five nations," the telegrapher charged.

Stone nodded. "And now we've got folks of every race, color, and creed settling up this country from those railroad cars."

The wagon driver had his team under control. They stood with heaving, foam-lathered sides.

"There ain't no settlers going to get off this telegraph wire from Fort Smith to Fort Sill," the telegrapher argued.

"No," Stone conceded, "but agent Nathan Able agreed to Chief Tsch-kote's request yesterday. He's ordered us to chop it down."

"What are you going to do about the railroad?"

Stone shrugged. "What are we going to do about the delegation in Washington that's arguing us Indians ought to take a little allotment of farm land and open up the rest of the Five Tribes reservations for settlement?"

"They call you the Five Civilized Tribes," the shotgun man said aggressively. "It's time you Indians lived up to your name and made way for progress."

"You'll have to drive on to Tsch-kotah Town and argue with old Sam. All we do is take orders," Stone said phlegmatically.

"I'll not waste a minute on Tsch-kote," declared the West

United troubleshooter. "We'll go back to Fort Smith and file suit against all five tribes and your Union Agency. The United States is entitled to set up lines of communication between its established forts."

The Seminole, Mutt Kiley, lifted a sack of makings from his blue Lighthorse jacket pocket and rolled a cigarette.

The telegrapher brandished his sawed-off shotgun. "And you'll let the rest of these telegraph poles stand. The more damage you do the more it is going to cost your people."

Mutt Kiley thumbnailed a match alight. Moving the match upward, he inhaled to ignite his cigarette, then casually, purposely, flipped the burning match toward the team of panting, febrile horses. As the blazing sulfur match flared toward the horses' heads they lurched back in the trace chains.

"Ho, there! Whoa!" shouted the driver, muscling the reins. But the arcing flame, the sawing reins, the driver's own impatient shouts, were too much for the harried team. They bolted.

The horses' sudden jolting spilled the shotgun man. He flung his arms upward, seeking balance, and triggered both barrels of the gun he clutched. The shotgun's roar spurred the runaway team. The double load of buckshot flew harmlessly off in the morning air as the gun's recoil tore it from the telegrapher's hands. It fell, bounding, in the dirt and the telegrapher followed it, falling out of the wagon.

The wagon was making way now as the shotgunner rebounded off its sideboards. He was barely able to catch the tailgate as the wagon flashed past him. Hanging on, he ran with giant strides to fling himself aboard among the strapped-down tools.

The shotgun was left lying on the ground as the wagon raced up the cut, over the rise and down into the draw beyond. Mutt walked over to pick up the weapon. He opened the breech and ejected the two fired buckshot shells.

"Mutt, you sure played hob," Millar Stone chided.

"Seminoles don't like being civilized," Kiley said. "It is a deadly ailment."

Stone was grinning. "So is monkeying with Mutt Kiley, I reckon. Well, anyway, you got yourself a sawed-off shotgun."

"And no shells for it," Kiley said. "But that's the Indian way—we always have just about half of what we need to make anything work."

Millar Stone removed his coonskin cap to scratch his scalp. "Well, them fellers are off in a cloud of dust. They'll raise some more dust when they get to Fort Smith." He stood thoughtfully. "I expect we'd better notify the Agency about this little fracas. Johnson, you ride down to Muskogee and tell Nathan Able. Mutt an' I will work on down the line with these tools of ignorance here." He picked up Johnson Lott's double-bitted axe.

"It's a good thing for them," Johnson Lott reasoned, "that shotgun just blew a hole in the air. Chief Tsch-kote and the Agency might take an even more serious view of a dead police-man or two than they do of these singing wires."

"I doubt it," Millar Stone said. "You better get on your way, boy."

Johnson Lott's horse Ceś-sē was worth the forty dollars the young Creek had paid for him, but not much more. The horse was a mouse-colored gelding standing fifteen hands high, and close to that many years in age. Ceś-sē's conformation was good, but somewhere in the past he had acquired the habit of sucking wind. While he was good for a short burst of speed, Johnson soon learned that he had to hold Ceś-sē in for the long haul.

But Johnson was not the kind to hurry. Raised in the old way, he knew he was not geared to compete, either with white men or with the acculturated tribal half-bloods—which made him more reticent. Accustomed to trying to remain incon-spicuous, his posture was often slumped, even in riding. His manner was always indrawn.

It nettled Johnson that beneath his dark-skinned reticence, pride burned. Living might be easier if he was not proud of being a full-blooded Creek, proud of his old-time Indian ways, proud of his people. He had joined the Lighthorse, providing his own horse and his gun, an ancient dragoon pistol. The pay was nearly nonexistent and irregular at that, but Lott knew the job he did was important.

It was about as close as a young Creek could come to being a warrior in this time of transition and the encircling influences of white men. It gave him the opportunity to ride with men he admired, like Mutt Kiley and Millar Stone—even if Millar was one-eighth white. Mutt was at least all Indian, being three-quarters Seminole and one-quarter Kickapoo.

The sound of their chopping axes was fading behind Johnson, slowly, for the chuck and thunk of a pair of chopping axes carries a long way in quiet, sparsely timbered country. Johnson rode at an easy pace, crossing the oak- and maple-timbered hills, listening to the conversation of a pair of crows that took turns informing everything within hearing distance of his progress.

By the time he had ridden out of earshot of Mutt Kiley and Millar Stone's labor the sun had passed its zenith. Johnson was glad that he was single and had no responsibility beyond himself, instead of a whopping big family to worry about, as Captain Stone did, or even just a wife and three young sons, like Mutt. It was afternoon and the crows, seeing that Johnson was leaving the country, gave up on him and went about their business.

A few meadowlarks protested his presence with their bright, twisting cries but, as the afternoon sun warmed, they too gave up, seeking solitude in grass-shaded retreats to rest up for the chore of chasing supper insects when the cool of the spring evening arrived. Johnson rode in quiet solitude. His horse's hoofs occasionally rustled last winter's leaves in the groves of trees, then became almost noiseless in the clear meadows of greening spring grass.

The country he rode came to parallel the course of the wide Arkansas River, shouldering well above it, then falling away gradually as he approached the Three Forks where the Arkansas, the Neosho, and the Verdigris Rivers join. He would not ride that far. The Agency stood on the hill west of the settlement that both Indians and whites called Muskogee. Muskogee was burgeoning now that it was a railroad town.

By midafternoon he was crossing the great flat plain of the river valley. Pecan trees, planted by the Creeks before the Civil War, were grown to maturity here. Johnson Lott remembered this pecan grove. It thickened as it approached the smaller stream ahead of him. Almost a river itself, it was called Ue-lau'kē by the Indians because it frequently overflowed its banks in times of heavy rains. Johnson knew that in a patch of high timber perhaps a mile west of the confluence of the Ue-lau'kē and the Arkansas, a deserted settler cabin was hidden.

Johnson knew the cabin was deserted because he and Millar Stone had served the papers on, and escorted out of the country, the squatter couple who had settled there—a dirt poor ex-Arkansawer named Coy and his snuff-dipping wife Ludy. It had been a mighty disagreeable assignment, but not a hard one. Everything the pair owned had been easily loaded in their wobbly-wheeled, dry-axled old spring wagon.

As the pecan grove through which Johnson rode gave way to native walnut and purple-leafed gum trees lining the course of the Ue-lau'kē, Johnson smelled smoke. It was late enough in the afternoon to be kindling a fire for supper, and Lighthorse policeman Lott thought, The Coys have come back. He reined to a halt. Sure enough, smoke. He touched his horse's mousy flanks and eased on through the openings between the towering trees.

He reached the narrow trace where Coy had hacked away the underbrush to make a wagon trail up to the cabin. Johnson recalled that the wagon trail branched off the old Texas Road, which passed nearly a mile to the west, then ran anti-goggling off toward the Red River. There were fresh tracks along the wagon trail, but they were not Coy's tracks. Coy's wagon tracks had been distinctive. They wandered; loose iron rims slipping, sliding, about to fall free of their dry wooden spokes and felloes.

These tracks were the symmetrical parallels of a larger, steadier wagon, one in good repair. Johnson could envision one of the high-sided emigrant wagons he had seen so often traveling south over the Texas Road. This one had wide iron tires, sweated tightly onto their rims, and they tracked in line with nary a wobble.

He paused to think this over. Either the Coys had fallen into good fortune since their escorted departure a couple of months ago or this was somebody new. If it *was* Coy, some risk was involved here. Coy was a wizened and bitter little man of Irish ancestry who had hotly resented being moved out. He insisted that this seemed like unused and unsettled country to him, where a poor man who had had hard years should have been able to make a home and scratch a living out of the ground.

His slatternly wife Ludy, with her snuff dipper's yellow, decaying teeth and her evil disposition, had been of the same mind as her husband. Johnson had seen their ancient family firearms, a rusty breech-loading rifle and an incredibly old flintlock, and if he rode up there alone he was sure to be recognized and might likely become the target of more than the Coys' waspish tongues.

It had to be looked into, though. Johnson rode Ceś-sē off the trail, hid him in a persimmon motte and proceeded up alongside the narrow trace, hanging back in the trees, until he sighted the cabin. The wagon, much as he had imagined it, stood in the yard. It was fairly new, its high sides scratched from passage through timber and brush. A lone mule set up a braying then from somewhere beyond the cabin and a man came outside to see what was causing the fuss. He was not the shriveled Irishman Coy, whose first name Johnson could not remember. This fellow was near six feet tall.

His standing slender and straight made him seem even taller, and Johnson figured him to be about forty-five years old, probably another Civil War veteran still looking for a place to light even though the war had ended years ago. Johnson remained unmoving in the edge of the timber. It takes sharp perception to see that which does not move, he knew, and the man who had stepped outside the cabin door, though looking around carefully, was not sufficiently alarmed to be more than normally curious. He walked around the side of the cedar cabin and Johnson could hear him talking pleasantly to a team of mules there.

He doesn't know that mule's language for "I smell an Indian," Johnson thought, as the man came back and again went inside the house. But I've got to find out who this jayhawker is, Johnson knew, so he turned back and eased feather-footed through the greening scrub along the edge of the trace, returning to Ceś-sē. This time he reined the mouse-colored horse into the faintly cut road, directly between the wagon's wheel marks, and rode on up into the clearing.

Thirty yards from the cabin he pulled up and called out, "Halloo, the house!"

Johnson saw quick and shadowy movement inside the open doorway, but the man did not come out. A girl did.

She was a slender girl. Tall, not exactly pretty, not exactly skinny, but pretty straight up and down. She had a clear complexion and a friendly face, so openly friendly that Johnson might have thought that she was bold had he not been able to see the plain innocence in her pale blue eyes. Johnson Lott felt his mouth open, like a carp in shallow water. He closed it again.

He had been all primed to talk to the middle-aged man, figuring to tell him as soon and as directly as possible that he was on Indian land, not welcome here, and how long did he intend to try to stay? But this thin girl, maybe twenty, as bright-eyed as a sunbeam slanting down through hazy timber air, left him dumbstruck. Floundering for a new mental foothold—Johnson Lott knew he was not facile of tongue—he opened his mouth, but it was her voice that broke the silence.

"My name is Martha Ann Lewis," she said, smiling as she enlightened him, but clearly not intending to embarrass him further in his discomfiture as she waited patiently for him to speak.

He did then. The words he got out were, "Your husband—"

"My father," she contradicted. "The mules seemed to be upset about something. He came out once and couldn't see anything, then he thought he'd better go back around and be sure their picket pins were set tight. It's probably a prowling skunk or something . . ."

The skunk is me, Johnson thought hesitantly. He was certainly conscious of his own dark complexion, of his scarred face, pitted from a childhood siege of chicken pox. Its pustules had left his skin pitted, if not pockmarked. The combination of his own and his horse's sweat, after the morning's work and the long ride in the sun, must have left him smelling as strong as a skunk if not quite the same flavor. She was so fine-featured she seemed pretty and, even from this distance, she smelled soapy clean.

Her father came back around the corner of the cabin's outthrust, scarfed and grooved cedar logs. He was carrying an armload of broken dry limbs, which he dumped beside the door.

"I see we've got company," he called out. There was friendly greeting in his voice. "That's what Jennifer was singing about. Get down," he invited, approaching Johnson's horse and holding out his hand. "I'm Silan Lewis."

Johnson leaned to shake hands, with a soft and gentle grip, as Indians do. "Johnson Lott," he said.

The white man responded gently, not trying to overpower his grip. "Get down," he invited again. "You've met my daughter. Supper is about ready."

Johnson looked down at his worn and saddle-wrinkled britches. He couldn't stay, but he kept looking at the girl and wanting to.

She said, "Yes. It's just a wild game stew and poke greens.

We won't even guarantee to fill you up, but you're welcome."

It occurred to Johnson that his duty as a Lighthorse police-man imposed on him the need to overcome his own timidity here. He was bound to find out more about this new squatter and his daughter. Finally, he said, "I'll ride down to the river and water my horse."

Martha Ann said, "I'll set another place."

Silan Lewis was nodding emphatically. "We'll be ready to eat by the time you get back here."

Johnson rode on through the clearing toward the river, ob-serving, and thinking about what he saw. The dooryard had been swept clean by a freshly tied bundle of hickory switches now hidden around the corner of the cabin, toward the horse lot. The litter of mule droppings in the horse lot told him that the Lewises' team had been penned there last night.

They were now staked out on picket pins beyond the pole corral, grazing on the young spring grass at the edge of the timber. Beneath the brush arbor that had sided the cabin for as long as Johnson had known it rested a moldboard plow, an iron-toothed harrow, and a growing heap of fresh-leafed branches Lewis had dragged in to repair the overhead of the arbor by replacing its dry branches. No, they were not just passing through. Yes, they intended to stay.

Johnson rode down to the Ue-lau' kē. He let the mouse-colored horse drink while he disrobed, hanging his clothes on the brush. Satisfying himself that the garments smelled more like sun than sweat, he figured that a little more sun wouldn't hurt them and he walked out over the flat shale of the stream bed, leading his mount. When the horse was belly deep he dropped the reins, moving on out in the chilly water until he reached swimming depth. Here he swam and washed, using the pebbles and clay of the stream bottom for soap.

The lithe, long-muscled Creek policeman then moved back to the bank, leaving the horse. Here, in shallow water, he squatted to wash out the drawers he had been wearing. He was flat-bellied, lean and waistless; muscles flexed and played across his broad shoulders as he wrung out the garments. Strong legs propelled him out on the bank, where he shook himself like a healthy young hound.

He hung the wet drawers on the bank brush and left them there while he whistled up his horse, dug clean underwear out of his blanket roll, dressed himself and rode back up toward the cabin. Fragrant smells of cooking floated down to him on the heavy evening air, starting his innards a-growling. He dismounted and off-saddled, racking his worn old kack and saddle blanket on the top rail of the pole corral, and walked on up to the cabin.

The door was closed now, so, holding in his hands his uncreased black hat with the long sweeping feather, he rapped diffidently on the lintel. He heard Martha's pleasant voice call, "The latch string is hanging on the outside," so he pulled it and entered. Then he stopped short.

Curtains hung at the windows. A red-checkered tablecloth covered the slab table. The earthen floor was neat and clean. The furniture they had brought in the wagon was already arranged. There was a chest of drawers, and two rope beds puffy with cornshuck mattresses and quilts. A pile of other belongings in the corner had been covered by another quilt. The wood Lewis had brought up was now stacked atop the woodpile beside the fireplace, in which a small fire of cooking coals glimmered.

The warmth radiating outward from the fire felt good to Johnson, for he was still shivering inwardly from his plunge in the cold stream, and the sun had fallen behind the high hills to the west. The evening was deepening into another chilly spring night. The girl and her father had been busy. Chinking and daubing had been replaced between the cedar logs around the fireplace, patching cracks where it had fallen out.

A little more work and the thick-logged cabin would be secure against the summer heat that was coming, and the winter cold beyond that. Johnson, impressed, said appreciatively,

"You folks are sure making improvements in this old hoot-owl hangout."

Silan Lewis's voice rose questioningly. "Oh? You're familiar with this place?"

Johnson nodded. "I've known it ever since Rufus Gromett and his hooligans built it to hole up in."

Martha Ann paused soberly at her table setting. "Do you suppose they'll come back here?"

"I expect not," Johnson reassured her.

Her father invited, "Hang up your hat and draw up a chair. Where is Gromett now?"

"Hanged," Johnson said. "In Fort Smith. He had a mixed bunch of outlaws—part Indian, part white, part black. They cut a bloody swath through here for a while. Held up a store over at Tsch-kotah. Ravished a farm woman a few miles north of here and killed her little boy. They finally caught up with them on the Texas Road down by Eufaula."

Martha was transfixed, her face firm. "Who caught up with them?"

"The U.S. marshals."

Silan Lewis moved the kerosene lamp from the fireplace mantel to the center of the table and sat down. "I've heard that this Indian Territory attracts riffraff from everywhere."

"Our Lighthorse police can't even arrest a white man," Johnson admitted, not knowing quite how to add that he himself was one of the officers so hamstrung.

"But the U.S. court for the western district of Arkansas does maintain jurisdiction here."

Johnson nodded. "Sometimes it stirs up more trouble than it settles, but the marshals and their deputies did catch Gromett's bunch. Took 'em to Fort Smith and hung them all at the same time—on Judge Parker's six-trap gallows."

The girl did not look relieved, just chalky-faced and grim as she nervously finished laying out knives and forks.

"Sit down, Mr. Lott," Lewis urged. "Our supper will be getting cold. Will you say grace?"

"Why . . . uh . . ." Johnson stammered, "as a matter of fact, I still belong to the square ground . . ."

Silan Lewis gave no indication of understanding, but did apparently sense the Lighthorseman's flustered reluctance and had no intention of embarrassing his Indian guest. He simply said, "I'm sorry," bowed his head, murmured a short grace and passed the steaming pewter container of stew.

Johnson regretted not having made some opportunity to relate his part in the removal of the Lewises' predecessors here, the Coys, and began to wonder how he might work back around to it. But Silan Lewis clearly had no intention of allowing long, awkward silences to develop around his dinner table. He was a genial host, relating tales of his Civil War service in General Blunt's army, and telling of the harassment of his family in Kansas by Jayhawkers and Quantrill's raiders.

"Both were predators," he declared contemptuously, "fighting for no one's benefit but their own. I returned to learn that my wife, Martha's mother, and my two young sons, Martha's brothers, were killed during the Quantrill raid in Lawrence. We could not stay there after that and, I'm sorry to say, have been wandering rather footlessly since. We tried farming in western Kansas, but that country is too dry. I heard that a commission in Washington plans to allot these Indian lands and open the rest for settlement. We decided we'd just as well get here for the opening."

Johnson sought a way to say that if his people had their way the commission in Washington would fail. There would be no allotment of Indian lands, and none left over for white "settlement." He was at the point of forcing the conversation back to the direction it should have taken and saying bluntly that it would likely fall his lot to have to escort them out of the Creek Nation as he had the Coys, when Martha Ann cut in, passing him the nearly empty bowl and offering, "You will have some more poke greens, won't you, Mr. Lott?"

Johnson looked at the smidgen left in the bowl. The thought

that he had already eaten more than a third of the food they could have split equally between them crossed his mind.

"No, ma'am, I couldn't eat another bite," he lied.

Her eyes were so blue, her slender face so finely made. Johnson took the bowl from her anyway and was overwhelmed by the incredible contrast between his long-tendoned, strong, dark hand and her long, slender hand, so cleanly pale pink, nearly white, with each pretty finger tapering to a silk-pink, neat-trimmed fingernail.

He set the bowl down, clumsily almost knocking over the sugar bowl, drawn again to those azure eyes so like these April morning skies, and said, "Folks, I've got to be on my way now."

Her pink lips parted to say, "Mr. Johnson, you'll surely stay the night and take breakfast with us."

Johnson Lott knew that no blush could tint his dark Creek cheeks, but if a redskin Indian could get redder he would have, for he was suddenly feverishly hot and sweating. "I thank you kindly, Miss, but—" It was an easy reach from where he sat to the peg by the door where his hat hung. His left hand pushed back the chair while his right swept the hat from the door peg and he backed out to retreat toward the horse lot.

Silan Lewis was not far behind. "I couldn't help noticing your horse this afternoon," he said. Near darkness had fallen. "He appears to be a fine animal."

"These mouse colors bottom out too quick for the kind of work we do," Johnson demurred. "Somewhere he's picked up the habit of sucking wind. See, he's doing it now." Johnson moved around to the gelding's head, stroking his muzzle to calm him.

"He thought he'd been put up for the night," Lewis guessed. "He doesn't like the idea of having to go on any further."

The horse was grunting, swallowing air, inflating his belly.

"You see he's angry," Lewis surmised.

Johnson nodded.

"He'll keep that up until he gets the colic." Silan Lewis

urged, "You'd better let him rest. Spend the night here. If he gets the colic you won't be going far anyway."

"I finally figured out a way," Johnson said. He extracted a straight pin from his hatband and rudely poked Ceś-sē's flank with it. The grunting and wind-sucking stopped. "It distracts his attention to some other part of his anatomy, I guess," the Lighthorseman explained. "Anyhow, it stops him before he gets the bellyache—"

Martha's frank but distinctly feminine voice said, "It seems a little cruel." She had followed them out, a barely visible shadow standing in the obscurity of the corral gate.

Her presence was surely disconcerting. Johnson hurried to apologize. "No, ma'am. If he gets the belly—the colic—he'll hurt a lot worse than that pin stick did."

Dimly, in the darkness, he could see her nod agreeably. "I know how stubborn a horse can be," she said. "I love to ride. We still have my mother's sidesaddle. It's among that truck in the corner covered up by the quilt in the house. I learned to ride astride, but Daddy says I'm a grown-up young lady now. He won't let me do that anymore. He always says he'd rather ride a horse than follow it with a plow, too, but farming has to be done on foot. What's your horse's name?"

"Ceś-sē," Lighthorseman Johnson Lott replied shyly, hardly knowing what to think about a girl so guilelessly talkative and frank. "Ceś-sē is a Muscogee Creek word for his mouse color." He gathered his saddle and blanket from the top rail of the corral, one-handed the blanket into place and threw the saddle across it, wondering what his Lighthorse partners would think of her, and of him—their supposedly stoic Creek warrior sidekick, standing around here in the dark stuttering and stammering, stepping on his own boot toes like a moony young buck sprouting green antlers. The Lighthorse catchers of bad men, earthy Millar Stone, strong Mutt Kiley, easygoing Lee Dewey . . . old Buck Tom would be grinning like a Choctaw chessy-cat . . . Johnson cinched his saddle around the gelding's belly and swung aboard.

"We hope we'll see you again," Silan Lewis invited warmly. "Yes. Indeed we do," Martha Ann echoed.

He nodded noncommittally and rode out of the yard. They would see him again, for certain, and under circumstances less social and delightful, for as soon as he told agent Nathan Able of their presence, Johnson knew, he would be riding straight back out here to evict them.

He swung down by the river to retrieve his cold, wet drawers, white patches in the dark night on the black lumps of bushes where he had left them. Then he cut Ceś-sē westward to the Texas Road and began the shallow climb up to Muskogee. Glumly, Lighthorse private Lott wished that there were Creek cuss words. He would have used some. Why did I do it? he demanded angrily of himself. Why didn't I have the guts to say what ought to be said? I could have got a tough duty over and done with.

CHAPTER 2

During two hours of black, moonless darkness, Johnson crossed the almost imperceptibly rising plain sheering off to the southwest of Muskogee and began climbing the sharply rising hill to the Agency. Near the top, the road bent and circled, so that he was less than a hundred yards from the big two-story Agency building before he could actually see it.

It bulked indistinctly against a few dim, distant stars, an official-looking structure where the agent and his family lived and worked in considerable isolation from the young town of Muskogee nearby. Somewhere far to the north, a grieving steam whistle wailed in brief loneliness. A decade ago, it would have been a steamboat bound upriver for Fort Gibson. Now, Johnson knew, it was a string of M. K. & T. freight cars huffing and puffing down from Pryor's Creek.

The Agency's darkness was complete. Everyone had gone to bed. He rode past the tall columns of the front veranda and around behind the big house. Beneath a towering maple tree he off-saddled and hobbled the gelding, then unrolled his blanket. Not ten yards from him, another sleeping lump snored. Another Lighthorseman ridden in late with some other information, Johnson figured, but he was too tired and disgusted with himself to try to figure out who. Let it wait until morning. On the opposite side of the tree from whoever it was, Johnson propped his head up on his saddle, covered himself to his nose with his blanket, and went to sleep.

When he awakened at first light his sleeping partner was already up and gone, but from the horse grazing alongside

Ceś-sē, Johnson knew his companion sleeper had been Leander Dewey, Chickasaw, from down Colbert's Ferry way.

There was lamplight in the big house's kitchen. Coffee, maybe even some breakfast. Johnson shook himself out of his soogan blanket, combed his hair with his fingers, rolled the blanket, carried it and his saddle around to the side porch of the Agency, and knocked. This was the entrance to the Agency office and when the door swung open in the hand of Nathan Able, Johnson could see Lee Dewey sitting beside the desk across the room.

Nathan Able, serious and already looking disturbed, managed a smile. "Come in, Private Lott. Go on into the kitchen and get coffee. We'll talk when you get back. There's bad news from Fort Smith." Able was a man of firm mouth, his face somewhat over-red from too much worry, his middle a little soft from too much desk work.

Johnson laid his saddle down on the porch with leather creak and wooden stirrup clatter and stepped into the office. Lee Dewey, blandly congenial, said, "Have Auntie Kerfetu wash your face and comb your hair while you're out in the kitchen." The Chickasaw was broad, tall, and muscular, with good humor in his flat voice. His eyes were a smiling betrayal of his sober mien.

"You bet, Lieutenant Dewey," Johnson said sleepily. "Everybody I come up against in this outfit who is senior to me gives me orders." As he crossed the office and entered the kitchen he thought, It sure didn't take those copper-wire stringers long to stir up a stink in Fort Smith.

The Creek Indian woman in the kitchen, tall and spinsterish, with a kerchief tied around her head, poured him a steaming mug of coffee without a word.

Johnson said respectfully, "They're not feeding you enough *sofkee*, Auntie."

"I'm not going to get to be one of those fat, lazy Indians," she said spiritedly.

Johnson went back into the office.

"Lieutenant Dewey has been over at Fort Smith trying to retrieve a Chickasaw they're holding for some trifling misdemeanor," Nathan Able told him. "He's got wind of an attempt by the Fort Smith marshals to take Catcher Twokiller while he's on trial at the Going Snake district courthouse."

So it wasn't the telegraph. Johnson recalled the Twokiller business. It was the current scandal of the Cherokee Nation. Catcher Twokiller had been feuding with an old man named Adler, a superannuated white man who had taken a young Indian wife. Twokiller had been calling on her, and the suspicious Adler had apparently decided to settle the matter with violence. Confronting the young pair during a tryst, Adler had aimed to shoot Catcher Twokiller, but his horse pistol was old and his aim was shaky. He missed. When Twokiller shot back, his aim was no better and he accidentally killed Adler's young wife, his own paramour.

"We're caught in a bind here," Able declared.

"Indians killing Indians is a tribal matter." Johnson sipped the scalding coffee.

"But an Indian shooting at a white man is a federal offense," the agent pointed out. "The U.S. government doesn't get upwrought over a dead Indian, even if she's young and pretty, but shooting at a lecherous old white man who has just tried to kill you is attempted murder. The Cherokee court can try Twokiller for accidentally killing his *inamorata*, but Judge Parker wants to try Twokiller for attempting to shoot old man Adler."

"Parker should be willing to wait until after the hearing at Going Snake courthouse," Lee Dewey said, peering into his empty coffee cup, "but the rumor is he won't. Our Fort Smith hanging judge has never been notable for patience. He wants to keep that six-trap gallows of his busy."

"The defense of the Cherokee Indian court," Nathan Able worried, "is the business of this Agency. If five or six federal marshals left Fort Smith yesterday, they will arrive at Going Snake courthouse today. I sent a runner south as soon as Lee got here yesterday evening. Millar Stone and Mutt Kiley should be arriving here right now. I don't know how my messenger managed to miss you on the way."

Johnson did not tell him. He sat in silence thinking, This is the time to say we have a new pair of squatters using the old Rufe Gromett cabin you had Millar and me run the Coys out of. But he did not say it. He sat daydreaming about Martha Lewis's frank and musical voice, her almost boylike slimness, and the pleasant meal he had enjoyed there.

Nathan Able even pressed him a little. "What are you doing here, Private Lott? Do you have some report about those telegraph wires being strung across the Creek country?"

I must have been swimming in the Ue-lau' kē about the time his messenger passed going south down the Texas Road, Johnson thought. He answered quickly then, giving a brief account of the encounter with the West United Telegraph men the previous day.

Agent Able sat listening, shaking his head. "Confound! Incredible! I've still had no word requesting right-of-way for a telegraph line, from the military or anyone else. Perhaps I shouldn't have been so precipitous as to agree with Tsch-kote that we should chop down those poles. I am usually more prudent."

He sat for a moment in baffled thought, then concluded, "We certainly have no time to concern ourselves with that now. It will take the four of you to confront this situation at Going Snake. The bureau authorizes each tribe to police its own precincts," he complained, "then refuses to allot money to hire enough Indian police to do the job. They assign one Lighthorseman from each tribe to this Agency and tell me to police more than fifty thousand square miles with them. Incredible is hardly the word . . ."

The door rattled. Through its frosted glass Johnson could see the stoop-shouldered form of Millar Stone, holding his coonskin cap in his hands, a shadowy Mutt Kiley standing behind him.

Dewey arose to open the door. "Mr. Able," he said soberly, "you ought to have some dogs around here. You need to keep these kinds of rascals from slipping up on you." Nathan Able rose momentarily to the bait. "When tribal people come here seeking help I certainly don't want to send them away dog-bitten—" He recognized the pair at the door then. His gray eyes passed over Dewey's poker face and he said, "Lee, I never know when you're hoodwinking me! Come in Millar, Mutt, we've been waiting for you. We must make smoke and talk."

The planning was short, for with no knowledge of what kind of situation might be encountered at the Indian court hearing of Catcher Twokiller no firm plan could be laid. Stone and Kiley did not even have time to unsaddle their horses. In less than half an hour the four Lighthorsemen were gathered under the maple tree where Lee Dewey and Johnson Lott had slept, getting ready to depart. Lee and Johnson were saddling their horses.

"How come you two slept out here on the ground?" Millar Stone asked. "Wouldn't Auntie Kerfetu let you uncouth Indians in the house?"

"I never sleep in a house if I can sleep outside," Dewey said peaceably. "White men's houses give me the dismals."

"I got here too late," Johnson said, and quickly changed the subject to avoid having to explain why. "I expect I would have spread my soogans inside the house if Lee hadn't already been snoring out here." He saw Auntie Kerfetu coming and kept on talking. "But it's true that Auntie Kerfetu has a streak of Creek cussedness in her. You know her whole name is *Huvn-wv Kerfetu Se-kot*, and that means she doesn't have a man and has never slept with one. It's no wonder, because the better you get to know her—"

The middle-aged Creek woman, wearing kerchief and brightly quilted jacket against the morning cool, took a long swing at the young Lighthorseman with the flour sack she carried. He ducked easily, and Millar asked, "Is that our grub?"

In sham anger she declared, "Frybread and fatback. And it's all you deserve! He's lucky I don't pour this boiling coffee down his back." She handed Captain Stone a crockery jug. Grinning, he tied it to his saddle horn. She handed up the sack, ordering, "Don't give that young Creek smart aleck any."

Johnson swung up into his saddle. "When we get back, I'm going to sleep in the house. Leave your door unlocked, Auntie."

The smile in her eyes was sardonic as she watched them ride out of the yard.

They rode slowly, pacing themselves carefully. "It's a long ways to Going Snake courthouse," Millar Stone reasoned. "We may get there too late. If we push these crowbait nags too hard, we may not get there at all."

They skirted through the sprinkle of weathered shacks that constituted Muskogee's north edge, making for the Three Forks ferry. It crossed the Arkansas River just below the mouth of the Neosho. The confluence of the narrower Verdigris was in sight a little farther upstream as the slow passage of their cable-drawn ferry barge stimulated further speculation.

"Boys," said Millar, "we are apt to get our tocuses shot off this time."

Johnson shrugged. "I guess we've got nothing better to do with 'um."

Mutt Kiley stood watching the swirling blue current of the river as the ferry crept slowly through it.

"No, Johnson, that's not right," he said thoughtfully. "All of us have family, except you."

"Even most of my ancestors died in the winter of '36, when the government was moving them out here," Johnson Lott persisted.

"Well, that's pretty much true of all of us," said Stone.

"My dad was killed in Florida. He was one of Osceola's warriors," Mutt said. "My mother froze to death on the way out here."

"I've been busy making a new family," Stone pointed out, "what with my wife and eleven kids, from the baby to young Millar, who's twenty-five. Now I've got five grandkids. There's young Millar and Malinda and Calvin. Blossom, she's my oldest girl, has got two. But all that don't make up for the old folks we lost. I guess I was about three when Andy Jackson's troops moved us west. That was more than forty years ago, and I can still remember how cold it was."

Mutt nodded. "A reason we honor the old folks so much is that there are so few of them. My three boys have no grandparents."

Millar remembered, "I guess there was about eighteen to twenty wagons in our particular bunch, herded by a troop of federal soldiers. It was in February, and you know how those snowstorms can hit in February. Everybody was weakened down by the weather, then the other side of Little Rock a spell of cholera hit us. Folks was dying like flies. Ten or a dozen a day. My folks, papa and mama, and three kids was all buried in one grave. I guess it's a wonder anybody lived, especially me. For some reason, I come through. The people that was left took turns raising us orphaned kids."

Kiley still stared into the passing water. "The trail where they cried."

"The trail of tears, the whites call it now," Millar said, "and they can speak mighty harshly about the way those Georgians took our property, our livestock, all under the aegis of a national hero, Andrew Jackson, 'Old Hickory.' "

The ferry was nearing the far side of the river. It butted the shallows, jarring horses and men, then slid up on the bank and they disembarked.

Mounting up, Dewey said, "My parents made it out here in pretty good shape. It was after they got here their troubles

started. They died when I was eleven. We always figured
someone poisoned them."

"Who?" Stone asked directly.

"No way of knowing," Lee Dewey conceded. "Probably
one of those squaw men who run cattle down there along Red
River. They try to keep the population thinned out and pick
up a little patch of land now and then. The times were so bad
even after I got married that I didn't want to have any kids,
but my wife persuaded me."

"How'd you manage to grow up?"

"My grandparents raised me." Dewey's mount ran friskily
out ahead of the others. The Chickasaw pulled him up, circled
and returned. "So I can't agree with you, Johnson," he added.
"I aim to try mighty hard to live long enough to raise my two."

"I wouldn't give too much for your chances," Johnson said
coldly. "Even nowadays you hardly ever see an Indian more
than forty years old, barring our captain, here. What with the
booze, and most don't eat right, and there's still the white
man's ailments. We do some things the Indian way, and some
the white man's way, which usually adds up to no way at all.
Some have hung on to their Indian names like cockleburs. The
rest of us have white man's names some Agency clerk or
schoolteacher give us. We ain't sure who we are!"

"We do the same thing with our kids," Millar admitted.
"Mamie 'n me give eight of ours white names, but three have
Indian names. No reason. Just happened that we did it that
way. We're mixed up all right, and this is getting mighty mor-
bid. After all, we all grew up to join the Lighthorse and draw
down these big wages and live this life of ease."

"You are right," said his lieutenant, Lee Dewey. "We ought
to be more cheerful. We ought to try to make Tahlequah by
noon, and the courthouse is almost thirty miles north of Tahlequah."

They rode silently for a while. Johnson began to feel guilty
because he had said nothing to the agent about the Lewises.
There just wasn't time, what with him being so stirred up

about the Fort Smith marshals and the Going Snake trouble, he alibied himself. He thought about Martha Ann, contemplating the fact that she was almost skinny, but his passing attempt to denigrate her did not override his memory of her azure eyes, the transparency of her complexion and her open countenance, so friendly and free of guile.

The horses, separating a little, alternately walked and cantered through greening meadowland. Their passage was hilly, but less timber-cluttered since they had struck northeast from the river, finally passing a good three miles south of Fort Gibson and continuing on toward the Cherokee capital.

The sun warmed and Johnson shed his faded blue uniform coat, tying it behind the saddle with his blanket. Mutt Kiley unwound his turban, carrying it looped over his arm, letting his long black hair blow in the wind for a while before he casually caught it up and began crisscrossing the turban layers around his head, letting the green and brown cloth loop gracefully down toward his shoulders on the sides, and finally leaving Johnson wondering how he was able to secure the spiraled cloth with no knots, no pins, and no beginning or end visible. Johnson knew that a good many Seminoles and a few of the die-hard older members of all the Five Tribes still wore turbans. But you saw less of them all the time and, thinking about it, Johnson preferred his hat—one of the few white-man things he really did prefer, he knew.

His horse was blowing a little now, a symptom of being windbroke, but some of it was pretense, the horse's protest against the steadiness of their travel. He slowed the blowing Ceś-sē down anyway, causing Captain Stone to comment, "Lee is the only one of us who's got a decent horse. You can't beat them Chickasaw horses."

Dewey's was a tall blood bay, with delicate ears, a long neck, a deep chest and a well-rounded rump, descendant of a long line of horses carefully Chickasaw-bred in colonial times by blending English and Spanish bloodlines. Lee made no attempt to hide his pride in the handsome, gaited bay.

He suggested whimsically, "Maybe I ought to ride on up there and reserve seats in the courthouse for you scissorbills."

Millar grumbled, "I'll be willing to set outside. To tell you the truth, I never heard of a errand more worthless. Catcher Twokiller is no more than a half outlaw. He ought to be in jail and I can't see that it makes any difference whether he is in the federal pokey at Fort Smith or the Cherokee National Jail in Tahlequah. Old man Adler is a horny old goat and a plain damn fool to have married a loose camp woman like that young chippy Tsi-ne-na. Who knows how many of them young Going Snake bucks have been chasing her—and how many was catching her. Even her name means 'Let's go.'"

The sun was close to the high-noon meridian as they rode through Tahlequah. Shade fell almost directly beneath the big trees around the two-story brick Cherokee capitol and at the feet of the statues of Adair and Stand Watie. The nooning glare lighted the face of the Male Seminary up on the hill. As they rode past the square, the several old-timers who sat palavering in the shade stopped talking to watch them ride by. Four Lighthorse policemen riding through town together was not a common sight.

There was no use stopping to ask if any Fort Smith marshals had passed through. The marshals might have ridden as far west as Sallisaw, but they would then have traveled directly north, and nowhere near Tahlequah. Johnson was certain that most of these Cherokee old-timers would know Millar Stone, too. They would be curious where the Lighthorse captain's posse was headed and what they were up to. But Millar did not stop to satisfy their curiosity. No use picking up any hangers-on either.

They crossed the Illinois River at Three Mile Crossing, went six more miles and turned northeast, following the course of the Baron Fork. When, after turning north from the river, they arrived at the courthouse, it was deserted.

The unimposing little one-room building of raw unfinished board and batten construction sat in the bottomland flat among fairly thick trees, not far from the Baron Fork. Going Snake courthouse looked more like an unused settler cabin than a courtroom.

A peter bird called disconsolately from the grove down a draw toward the river. There was not a human in sight in any direction. It was two-thirty in the afternoon. The Lighthorsemen pulled up their ponies and sat, loosely grouped, puzzling the situation. Mutt Kiley rode a circle around the courthouse, studying the leaf mold that littered the ground.

He returned to say, "There's been nobody here today, or for two or three days."

Millar Stone said, "That's odd." He sat pensively, resting his hands on his saddle horn. "Do you reckon we got here on the wrong day? Maybe Nathan—"

Lee Dewey was shaking his head. "No," he said. "I was told that Judge Parker himself handed down the order. He told Marshal Fletcher Parr to get his men together and serve the writ while the trial was in progress. This was the day. Parr was supposed to demand custody of Catcher Twokiller, arrest him on a charge of attempting to murder Adler, then bring his prisoner back to Fort Smith."

"Then he has sure done it on a magic carpet," Stone declared. "We can get down here and wait for a while. Maybe somebody will come along who can tell us what kind of medicine they made." He stepped down off his horse. So did the others. Stone stood holding his reins. "Scatter out and see if you can find any sign, boys. I never heard of Cherokees holding a court hearing they didn't start early in the morning."

The four scattered, afoot, leading their horses, going beyond the circle Kiley had ridden. Johnson knew the Seminole would have missed nothing in the area he had searched. Apparently Stone and Dewey were of the same mind. Johnson descended into a draw, then angled upward from its moist depths. Shallow gray limestone ledges lifted outward from the upgrade here, ending in a rubble of sterile caliche. Ascending the bare rock slabs, in clear sight of the rustic Going Snake courthouse, Johnson reached the point where his eyes were level with the caliche rubble, and he stopped short.

Studying the loose rock momentarily, he took another step, then quickly turned to retrace his way. A sizable bunch of horses had milled in that caliche fairly recently. It was hard to say how many hours ago, but there were still places where iron-shod horses had scuffed the rocks, leaving sharp scar marks that had not lost their edges. He would get Captain Stone, let him take a look-see—

A rattle of distant shots silenced the peter bird. Johnson froze, listening, and staring at Going Snake courthouse. Dewey, Kiley, and Stone were all in sight, about equidistant from the raw slab court building, scattered among the thick trunks of trees and greenery of the flat. Each stood, statue motionless, listening. The chatter of gunfire recommenced, far away, but ricocheting clearly through the park in which they stood.

The faint gunfire stopped as abruptly as it had commenced. There were three more isolated shots, so distant as hardly to disturb the quiet of the spring afternoon, then all sprang into motion. Millar Stone, farthest to the north, was swinging into his saddle. His arm lifted in a long, beckoning sweep. Lee Dewey, already mounted and riding, had almost reached his side.

Mutt Kiley, pausing in mid-stride to glance back at Johnson, had thrust a moccasin in a stirrup, his paint horse caracoling as he held him in, giving Johnson a chance to catch up and not fall too far behind. Ceś-sē splashed across the muddy bottom of the draw. Lighthorseman Johnson Lott urged the gelding forward eagerly, muttering, "Don't start sucking wind now, you welsher." Stone and Dewey were already out of sight.

Kiley could apparently see them. Johnson could not, but he could still see Kiley's back as he leaned forward above the bouncing of his horse's long, jumping strides. The Seminole rider held his place midway as the run lengthened into minutes. Now Johnson could see Mutt fighting the head of his overanxious mount, slowing its charge.

After six minutes, maybe half a minute more, of all-out run, Johnson felt a slight rise of pride in his mouse-colored horse. He had kept up the pace. There were men up ahead, partisans in rough frontier garb. Some of them were milling around, some were just standing. A group was beginning to gather around Stone and Dewey. Kiley still fought the reins to bring his own excited horse to a halt, then stepped out of the saddle to join the gathering.

The log house standing alone on the knob must be a schoolhouse, Johnson thought. It looked like a schoolhouse, with a pump in the yard and two small backhouses with separate paths running to them out behind. People were still straggling down the front steps out of the schoolhouse. Two men were carrying a third man, lugging him by armpits and ankles. He hung limp between them and they laid him on the ground, distractedly, in the sun.

Johnson rode on up but stayed in his saddle. The milling, both men and women, was still going on. Some still wandered, either toward or away from the schoolhouse, and some just stood. The clot of people gathering around the dismounted Lighthorsemen was growing. Several of them were talking and Johnson began to pick up words and phrases. "Judge Valley had moved the hearing up here to Going Snake schoolhouse because he thought the school would be more defensible," a hawk-nosed part-Indian man was saying. So they must have had some premonition of trouble, Johnson thought.

A woman, near hysterics, cried out shrilly, "The first I knew anything was happening I heard one of the men at the front door say, 'Come in, gentlemen,' to the marshals, I guess, then they were shooting all around me . . ."

". . . it was deafening . . ."

". . . my ears are still ringing . . ."

". . . you can see this powder burn here on my face . . ."

Johnson began to count the others who lay on the ground.

Besides the man who had been carried from the schoolhouse and laid in the sun, there were nine. Each had one or more people leaning or working over them. Indian women were crying and wailing. A covey of Cherokee men, carrying firearms, had begun to move down toward the foot of the hill. They hesitated, then returned, heading toward the tie rail that ran along the south side of the log building. A few buggies, other vehicles, and saddled horses were secured to it.

"That's old man Adler over there." The hawk-nosed man pointed to one of the bodies on the ground.

The group returning up the hill approached the tie rail and began loosening their horses. Millar Stone looked around quickly and told Johnson, "Ride over there, Private Lott, and tell that bunch to stand pat."

Johnson appraised the group as he cantered toward them. They were all full-blooded Cherokees. He knew they would not be overly eager to take orders from a Creek younker like himself, so, on reaching them, he politely asked, "Wait a minute. Captain Stone is on his way over here. He wants to talk to you."

He rode back to Stone. Someone was angrily declaring, "They shot first—" Johnson interrupted to say, "Captain, maybe you'd better not wait too long before you say something to those fellows over there."

Stone hesitated, then walked, plodding and obstinate, over to the group of Indian men now ready to depart. Johnson dismounted to follow, leading his horse.

Stone confronted the group, blocking their way. "Now the best way I can get it," he addressed them, "the marshals just rode up and came walking in—"

"They weren't marshals," a husky Cherokee, his face suffused with hot blood, contended. "Just Fletch Parr. The rest were whites and half-breeds from around here. Sidekickers of old man Adler. One of them shot Catcher Two-killer, my brother's son, as soon as they came in. Now my nephew is dead."

It was an openly partisan crowd, and Johnson recognized it clearly. The clot of men and women who had first gathered around Millar and Dewey obviously represented the other side. One of those standing around Dewey, halfway down the hill, declared loudly, "Católo, Judge Valley, would just have let Catcher go. The trial would have come to nothing."

The Cherokees beside the hitching rack were mounting their horses and the latent foreboding in the air intensified. Still Millar Stone stood obdurate, a stoop-shouldered, stubborn man, even appearing flat-footed in his clumsy Agency-issue brogans.

"How many of your people are laying on the ground?" he asked the mounted party.

"Five. Judge Valley and Catcher Twokiller are in the schoolhouse. Fletcher Parr is in there, too. The judge was shot in the breast and he is dead by now."

Johnson thought, Maybe you'd better let that bunch ride on off to wherever they're going, Millar, before we're all laying dead on the ground.

Stone walked toward Dewey and the opposition party. "How many of your bunch is down?"

The hawk-nosed leader replied, "Seven." He looked more Yankee than Indian. Maybe he was a relative of old man Adler's.

Stone stopped in the middle, eyeing the opposing forces. "Don't the both of you reckon that's enough?" His obsidian eyes were hard and shiny. "Where do you aim to go?" he asked the mounted full-bloods.

"After those marshals they trumped up," grunted their husky leader. Johnson saw that he wore a straight pin in the lapel of his linsey coat. He was a pin Indian—a member of the Kee-to-wah, a bringer of the eternal fire, one of the full-blood outfit accused of ancient tribal assassinations.

"Those marshals ain't trumped up," Stone said. "They may be folks that you consider enemies, from right around here. But they're marshals, all right. Duly sworn in as deputies by

United States Marshal Fletcher Parr. You take out after them, you're chasing authorized officers of the law engaged in the discharge of their duty pursuant to a legal writ handed down by the federal court in Fort Smith."

He turned his lecture on the opponents of Catcher Two-killer, the supporters of old man Adler. "You folks have got yourselves in a fix. Altogether, from both sides, twelve are already dead, including a U.S. marshal. More of you are wounded. Which side do you figure is the winner in this mess?"

Accusations began to fly back and forth.

"The federal posse tied up their horses in that little fringe of trees down there. They just walked in and started killing people!"

"Catcher Twokiller shot first," declared an Adler partisan.

"I saw him shoot," an Indian woman confirmed. "He shot my cousin, John Ga-na-ge, point-blank, right in the face!"

"They were so close together in there their gun barrels touched the people they were shooting."

"Boom! Bang! Blooey! I never heard such a noise." The woman who had said it before repeated, "My ears are still ringing!"

The shouting became random, first one and then another calling out.

"I ran outside. Somebody was shooting a shotgun right behind me."

"The whole fight ran outside. A bullet went by my ear. From one of the marshals' carbines, I think. It screamed like a big saw cutting through a hickory knot."

"And Judge Valley moved the trial up here because he said he thought it would be easier to fight them off from this log schoolhouse than from that little slab courthouse down by the Baron Fork!"

"You can't fight them off when they're already among you like wolves! And shooting at the same time!"

Johnson kept his hand on his gun, in case someone started

shooting again. He could see that Mutt and Lee were maintaining the same watchful caution.

"Judge Valley wouldn't have done anything anyway."

"That's why he wanted the trial in Indian court. He was afraid Judge Parker would hang Catcher in Fort Smith."

A Twokiller partisan yelled, "Indian trials are for Indian courts. Our treaty guarantees it!"

Millar Stone stopped it. "Nobody can fight each other harder than us Indians ourselves. All this yelling isn't doing any more good than the shooting did. Look around you. Relatives are grieving over these people on the ground who are not alive anymore. What do you get out of yelling at each other? Or killing some more? This is enough. You folks scatter out and go home. You're not going to settle anything here. Take those who are dead and hurt with you. Me an' the Lighthorse will stay here with those who have no one to watch out for them."

There turned out to be just one. The four Lighthorsemen began moving about in a businesslike way, helping Cherokees, whites, and half-bloods. With the emotional fervor quieted, in the shock of loading up the dead and wounded, even the most militant became gradually passive. Numbed, even the combatants were helping each other. Johnson followed Millar Stone into the schoolhouse. The body of Judge Valley, bald-headed, old, and grossly fat, lay beside the teacher's desk. Confronting it, across the small table where the defense had sat, slumped the young antagonist, Catcher Twokiller, waxen in death.

One of the Adler partisans asked, "What about . . . him?" He pointed to Marshal Fletcher Parr, lying beside the door in a pool of his own blood.

"We'll take care of him," Millar said.

First the lone riders, then the wagons, pulled out in various directions. When the school grounds were quiet and deserted, Lee Dewey stood on the schoolhouse's front stoop. "What a carnage," he said. "And why?"

A groan, sepulchral and hollow, came through the door. He

spun to reenter the schoolroom and as Millar, Mutt, and Johnson followed they found Lee kneeling with his ear on Fletcher Parr's chest.

Parr sat up, and the Lighthorse captain marveled, "Dang if them Fort Smith gunslingers aren't hard to kill!"

The bullet that had opened the long wound in the marshal's temple, above his right ear, had caused copious bleeding, but he was still alive, his eyes open and wondering.

"Well, to sort of answer your question, Lee, and any you might have, Fletch," Millar commented, "old Adler, Catcher Twokiller, the judge that convened this hearing, and most of the deputies you swore in to interrupt it are killed. There may not be any need for more litigation because it's going to be hard to find anybody to charge. Let's bandage him up, boys."

His head so swathed in white that he had to carry his own hat in his hand, Fletcher Parr insisted that he was well enough to ride. The burly, rough-faced marshal thanked the four Lighthorsemen profusely for looking out for him, walked to the fringe of trees at the edge of the clearing where his horse was tied, mounted, and rode off.

Nathan Able sat mute at his desk, distressed, but hearing Stone's report out in its entirety. Only after a long and thoughtful silence did he comment. "There is certain to be a congressional investigation of this whole tragic imbroglio. There is enough wrong, and enough right, on both sides that I doubt any official action will ever come of it. But I'll wager Fort Smith interrupts no more Indian trials so roughly."

Johnson, his gaze fixed on the horizon beyond the office window, contemplated the dilemma. By the treaty made following the Civil War, Five Tribes Indians were entitled to keep the peace within their own territory. Conflict resulted because no Indian officer could arrest any white man on any charge. Indian courts could try only Indians; the federal court had jurisdiction where whites were involved. Old man Adler had been white. Even though Tsi-ne-na had been killed when old man Adler had been shot at by Catcher Twokiller, the federal court considered the missing of Adler more important than the killing of Tsi-ne-na. She was Indian. Painfully aware of this dichotomy, they still had to live with it. Another current example was whiskey.

As if he had been following Johnson's thoughts, Millar Stone said, "I expect we might as well hunt firewater for a while then."

Able nodded. "There is still much agitation over the allotment issue. The Crazy Snakes down by Eufaula are the main agitators, and booze is their major stimulus. I'm getting reports that they're threatening any Creek who accepts an allotment, and warning Indian ranchers not even to hire a white cowhand. We've had reports of haystacks being burned, along with one house down by Tamaha. Whiskey just seems to drive them wild."

"You have to figure," Millar cautioned, "when a white man drinks whiskey it removes a layer or two of his civilization. You remove a layer or two of some of these Indian's civilization, an' there ain't any civilization left."

Nathan Able nodded. "The white man is supposed to have been civilized for centuries," he agreed. "The veneer of Indian civilization is only a couple of generations deep. We've got to get this whiskey situation pinned down."

"What about the telegraph lawsuit over in Fort Smith?"

Able smiled ruefully. "What with the bootlegging, and allotment on the horizon, no tribal funds, children needing education, and old folks needing medical care, who has time or strength left to worry about a lawsuit? Let them sue! You can't get blood out of a turnip."

The agent stood up, "You ride on back up into Cherokee country, Millar. Johnson take the Creek Nation: Leander and Mutt into the Chickasaw and Seminole. I'll get word to Buck Tom down in the Choctaw Reservation. Let's ferret out the stills and the whiskey runners. If they're Indian, arrest them and spill their merchandise. If they're white, come and report them to me."

Johnson wandered on out into the kitchen. Going back into their home country would give Mutt and Dewey a visit with their families and Millar a few days with his growing clan of sprouts. Johnson wondered who he might visit, and a vague notion passed through his mind. Auntie Kerfetu was baking sweet rolls. Johnson stole one.

"Policeman," she smirked scornfully, and added, "Thief!"

He winked and took a conscience-free bite. "Don't Mr. Able's wife ever work around here?"

"She teaches the kids, I do the cooking." Auntie motioned toward the double kitchen windows.

Johnson went to stand before them. In the heavy shade beneath the maple tree where he and Dewey had slept sat a circle of some thirty youngsters—Indians, blacks, and whites. They ranged in age from six or seven to teenagers. Mrs. Elizabeth Able sat in the center of them. Her long hair was pulled back and firmly braided into a neat bun. Slates and chalk indicated that the teenagers were doing sums. Mrs. Able read aloud to a segment of smaller children on the periphery of the circle.

"Where do you reckon a thirsty man would find a jug of whiskey, Auntie?" Johnson asked.

She made the chirking noise of shame. "That, and thieving," she chided.

Johnson turned around. She was wiping her flour-whitened brown hands on a dishcloth. His suspicion was that she knew every particle of gossip in the Creek Nation. Any Indian who came calling on the agent and brought his wife was providing a potential storehouse of information, for the women gathered in the kitchen and talked while the men conducted the tribal business.

"Not just one jug," said the Lighthorseman. "I need a whole passel of them."

She shook her head reprovingly. "You look like a long toper."

"I don't aim to guzzle 'em all," he demurred.

She stepped closer. "I have been feeding some blue jays here in the yard, and they tell me things. You know how noisy they are. One of them has told me that the place to find firewater is in that Younger's Bend down along the Canadian around Porum. Some white man is making it there."

Johnson made an appreciative mouth, licked the sweet frosting off his fingers, and went out the back door. Auntie Kerfetu's voice followed him outside. "I hope you find all you can drink," she called out ironically. "The birds say smoke often rises from a draw by the big spring there, and sometimes you see thirst-crazed snakes wriggling along the ground toward the head of the draw."

He took three days in riding south, pausing for a day at Webbers Falls. Riverboats coming up the Arkansas sometimes came carrying contraband whiskey. He watched a small steamboat buck its way up over the shallow water of the falls, remembering when they used to stop all the boats at Fort Coffee. Often the captain himself did not know his boat was carrying whiskey. Some enterprising crewman would just cache a few gallons in nets slung underneath the craft.

As the shallow-draft steamer made its laborious way through the white water of the rapids and the low, rocky falls, it scraped and grounded, off-loaded a few tons of general merchandise and dry stores, loaded again, and struggled on upstream, bound for the boat landing at Muskogee. Johnson let it go. There was no chance that liquor had been netted to the bottom of that boat. The rock groundings would have broken every jug and bottle.

The third day he rode on to Tamaha to look for the burned house. He did not find it. Andy V'lkan, a half-blood Creek rancher, showed him burned pastures and haystacks, and told him the Crazy Snakes had *threatened* to burn his house down. Andy favored allotment.

"The only way I can breed up any herd," he contended, "is to get an allotment in my own name. I'll fence it horse high, hog tight, and bull strong. The way things are now my cows have to run on open range, and they breed with every scrub bull that is running loose. Every year I get a crop of scrub calves."

Johnson listened and rode on. No matter how you slice anything, he thought, it still has two sides. He opposed allotment. Having been brought up in the old, traditional Indian ways, he felt the land belonged to all Indian people. As the tribal elders insisted, and Johnson agreed, the earth mother was not meant to be cut up into parts. What kind of children would want to cut their own mother up into parts so each of them could have a piece of her?

The way things are now, Johnson reasoned, Indians who believe in Indian ways have a chance to keep on living the old way, keeping the old customs, the honored ceremonials. Allot the land, parcel it out, and open the rest to white settlers and every Indian would be surrounded by white neighbors. The pressure to quit Indian ways and adopt white man's ways would become intolerable.

Now, at least, you can run the white settlers out of Indian Territory, escort them to the border. He stopped short, remembering Silan and Martha Lewis. As soon as he finished this present chore he had to ride back up on the Ue-lau' kē and warn them that they must leave.

He was approaching the Canadian River now, and crossed it just below where it flows into the Arkansas. Here was Pleasant Bluff, where General Stand Watie's Confederate Rifles had ambushed and captured the steamboat *J. R. Williams* during the war. Johnson pulled Ceś-sē up atop the high bluff and sat easy in the saddle, surveying the broad, sanguine river where it curved gracefully up against the bluffs. He sat imagining the fighting that day, when the Cherokee general had sunk the steamboat to the waterline with artillery fire from yonder on the far bank. Then he had proceeded to loot her treasure store of supplies until a Union Indian regiment had appeared to drive the Rebel Indians off from this bank. Watie's Cherokees had set the steamboat afire before retreating, and having unloaded enough of her stores to float her, left her to drift off the sandbar and downstream with the rest of her cargo burning. It had been a big victory for the Confederate Indians. Johnson hoped he was on the verge of a big victory as he rode on west, recrossing the Canadian at Briartown. Now, stealthily, he began his approach into Younger's Bend from the south.

CHAPTER 3

The timber was as thick as any through which he had ever ridden. It was big timber, not scrub brush or shinnery, a dense forest of deciduous trees blending into longleaf pines, with trunks twice the size of the telegraph poles they had enjoyed such healthful exercise in chopping down a while back. As the country rose the pines became taller, reminding him of the robbers' cave country in the San Bois Mountains farther south, where he knew Belle Starr and her outlaws often camped after their forays rustling cattle, stealing horses, and raiding the mercantile stores in the isolated little settlements of the territory.

He spent most of a whole day ascending the succeeding eminences of this climbing country. Then, getting down off Ceś-sē, he shinnied bearlike up one of the tallest trees to survey the ebb and flow of the terrain. Johnson was looking for smoke. In the late afternoon, along toward evening, he found it. Rising thinly into the high-country air above the meander of a valley cut into the darkly forested, mountainous hills.

The smoke was so thin it almost disappeared in the blue ozone atmosphere of the serried hills before flattening out to become slightly more visible. There, like the base of a light cumulus cloud, it rested on the denser air cushion of the earth beneath. Johnson climbed higher, to where the tapering trunk of the pine began to sway precariously under his weight. Here he clung to the rough conifer's bark while he committed to memory the necessary distances, directions, and landmarks. Then he shinnied down.

Riding again, he studied the drainage patterns, finding the

creek bed that emerged from the coulee he sought. It was dry, as he had suspected it would be. Considerable rain would have to fall high up, exceeding the needs of the forest floor at the head of the canyon, to create enough overflow to drain off through this shallow ravine. A torrent would then pour down through this run, strewn with its jagged rocks.

As Johnson proceeded up the dry wash, the gorge narrowed, becoming a high-walled draw, and here there was evidence on the bed rocks of a foreign substance. A faint, floury residue, carried down on some past freshet, clung to the rocks, turning to dust where he touched it. Johnson, dismounting, scraped some up on a finger to taste and smell it. Funny, he thought. Most bootleggers would feed remaining mash to their cattle, making the most economical use of the by-product of their sourmash corn whiskey. This fellow must have been caught in a deluge, or had an accidental spill. Or maybe he was just wasteful, or careless.

He swung back up on Ceś-sē's back and proceeded up the wash, leaning out of the saddle, watching and reading every mark on the rocks. Johnson figured he would have to ascend clear to the head of it so, presently, he rode the gelding into a thick undergrowth of seedling pines, dismounted, tied his horse, and proceeded on foot.

He heard it before he saw it, the musical dripping and trickling of spring water into its rocky basin. Yep, there it was, an ever-flowing cold-water spring running into its catch pool beneath the mossy earth and gray limestone overhang. The still was well situated, on flat slabs of stone beside the water-course where it ran out to sink from sight among pebbles a few yards downhill from the spring pool.

It was a complete layout—barrels of fermented mash, a big copper cooker, a condenser tank, then copper tubing running off through the cold trickles of the spring to a keg collector vat. The cooling, dripping springs helped condense the distilled steam from the cooker into the final liquefied product. At the same time, the steam in the coils was preheating the never-failing supply of pure water to serve the boilers. Ingenious and efficient—and running full blast! A crackling fire of cured pine logs snapped and popped hotly beneath the copper cooker.

Johnson lay still in the concealment of tumbled boulders thirty yards below the still, studying the whole array, and wondering where the bootlegger was. That his own approach, as cautious as it had been, had frightened off the whiskey maker was evident. He was nowhere in sight. How far the invisible bootlegger had gone, Johnson decided, depended on how frightened he was. If he was scared enough, he could be half a mile away by now and still running. Experience had taught Johnson that security gets mighty important to the guilty. They ran like hell for safety and deep hiding when they were sure a Lighthorse policeman had caught their scent. So he lay and listened.

Except for the dripping spring water, there was not a sound —not even a bird chirp or a squirrel bark. Johnson felt a little abashed. Maybe I'm losing my knack, he thought. He had always been a good stalker. I ought to be able to come through back country as dense as this without shutting up every wild critter that climbs, crawls, or flies. I was so hot on the trail I must have forgotten some of my own traveling manners.

He thought this over. I know where it is now—maybe I ought to ease out of here and come back with Millar and Mutt and the whole bunch. They're looking over their own country though, and not likely to holler for help from me. No, he decided, they'll kill their own snakes. I wish there was some way to fetch this snake out into the open. But if he has hunted his hole he may be so deep in that *cetto* there is no hope of fetching him out.

Johnson pulled his worn dragoon pistol from its holster, dreading the powder burns that always peppered his arms and face when he fired it. Holding it in both hands, at arm's length, he drew a careful bead on the copper cooker. A few bullet holes in the cooker, the condenser tank, and the vat seemed like a good way to start.

"Uh-uh." The softly spoken negative came from behind him, to the left.

Johnson knew better than to make any fast or sudden moves. He held his aim on the cooker and turned his head, slowly, until he could see the *kawnakausha* sitting on the rocky eminence to his left. The *kawnakausha* name came to his mind unbidden, and it seemed well chosen, although Johnson could not recall having ever heard that any of the little people were white. In all the *kawnakausha* tales he'd heard in being passed from family to family while growing up, the fairy folk had always been Indian.

This one was white—a gnarled little white man as bald as a May apple. He was grinning wickedly and clinging to a .50-caliber Sharps rifle that was taller than himself. The long rifle lay across the flat rocks, pointed carefully at the prostrate Lighthorseman's rump. The little man wore ragged clothing— at first glance his garments seemed like patches sewn on patches.

He still grinned evilly, yet somehow half pleasantly, and Johnson Lott had not even the slightest doubt that, at any careless movement on his part, the bald-headed white man, without losing his evil grin, would carelessly blow a hole in the seat of Johnson Lott's pants and rake his back with those big Sharps slugs.

The little man nodded. "From your rump to where your shoulders hump."

Johnson squirmed. He was used to Millar Stone reading his mind, but it irritated him that a white man could do it. Carefully, leaving the dragoon pistol laying out there as far as his arms had reached with it, Johnson cautiously rolled over and sat up.

He leaned back, bracing himself with his palms against one of the creek-bed boulders. "Who in tunket are you?" he asked.

"My family name I gave away, so them as wants calls me Bluejay," the elflike man singsonged.

Johnson shook his head. "It's no wonder the birds talk about you! How'd you sneak around behind me and get the drop on me?"

"I'm a wizard. I turned myself into a lizard."

His versified speech was beguiling. Johnson relaxed a little. "How come you didn't throw down and shoot me on sight?"

"A bullet barricade would hurt my trade. At first I thought, 'A customer!' But now I think, 'A Lighthorse cur!'"

Johnson scrutinized the bootlegger soberly. He was a white man all right, and short—maybe an inch or two under five feet. He was fully bald, with eyebrows so white he almost appeared to have none, and chilly gray eyes. An eccentric old codger, sure enough—but maybe that's what it took to live back in the hills and make whiskey for Indians. Auntie Kerfetu had said he was a squaw man—a white man married to a Creek woman —which was why he felt safe here.

"Old man," Johnson warned, "you know what you're doing here is illegal, against tribal law, and you can't keep on getting away with it."

"You preach on me, I'll tell the agent soon of thee—and Martha Lewis, the squatter's daughter—you think of her more than you oughter!"

Johnson smothered his sudden risibility and shook his head, almost disbelieving. He squinched up his dark eyes, thinking hard, then said, "It does appear, and I'm sincere, you've got me here, and you'll prevail. I guess I'd better hit the trail."

Bluejay nodded enthusiastically. "It's as you say. Just don't come back another way, or bring your friends some other day."

Johnson reached, cautiously, to retrieve and slide his dragoon pistol into its holster. He stood up, dusting the rock residue from his hands, and started walking down the ravine. Outside of a peculiar hollow sensation in his back, as if it already had a bullet hole in it, he felt no noteworthy fear. As he stiff-legged his way down the steep wash, taking care not to slide and fall on a loose slab or a rolling rock, he got, not a bullet, but another verse.

"Lighthorse policeman Johnson Lott, use what brains as you have got. Hear what I say, take my advice, and freeze your tongue as if 'twere ice."

Johnson did not turn to look back, but raised his arm in farewell salute and turned off into the pine scrub to climb aboard Ceś-sē. On his way north, past Tamaha, Pleasant Bluff, and Webbers Falls, through three days of riding, he ran the strange experience back and forth through his thoughts. Auntie Kerfetu had said that blue jays squawking in the yard had told her of the whiskey still operating at Younger's Bend. The odd little bootlegger had called himself Bluejay.

Fighting down deep-seated old Indian superstitions as best he could, Johnson could not quite force from his mind a wondering: Could this pixified old man who called himself Bluejay really be a *kawnakausha,* a Choctaw-breed leprechaun? His still *was* snuggled right up to the edge of Choctaw country. He had known Johnson's name, and his purpose in being there as a Lighthorseman. He had divined Johnson's thought about being shot in the rump by the Sharps big fifty, and most astounding of all, he had known about Martha Lewis.

The Lighthorse policeman instincts in him then gravitated toward sensibility and he rationalized that Auntie Kerfetu probably knew Bluejay's Creek wife and felt sorry for her. That train of reasoning led to other disturbing thoughts then, and his face turned warm, then hot, as he realized and admitted to himself where he was heading. He excused this with the pretense that he felt sorry for Martha Lewis.

It was hardly any revelation to realize that he had been traveling toward the Lewis cabin ever since leaving old man Bluejay's still. He was bound for Nathan Able's office at Muskogee, and the Lewis place was on the way. Surely, before going on to report their presence to the agent, he should stop and see if they were still there. He ought to defy Bluejay's threat and his own emotions, whatever they were, and report the Lewises. What was revealing, and wiped out all pretense, was that he knew he had no intention of reporting their presence at all.

He agonized about this a little, for he could not reconcile his attitude and his intentions with his duty as a Lighthorseman. Johnson could not comprehend his outlandish feelings about Martha Lewis. She was a white girl. He was a Creek full-blood, deeply immersed in Creek tribal beliefs, convinced of the rightness of the old ways. Instinct urged him to find a refuge, a place in which to study all this through to a logical conclusion. The Lewis cabin was where the major ingredient that inspired all this turmoil was to be found. There he could see the elements involved in reality rather than only in his imagination. It seemed the ideal place to decide what he ought to do.

When he arrived at the cabin he found Martha herself in considerable turmoil. In her thorough cleaning of the cabin she had found some scraps of paper. They looked official and she thought they might be important, even though somebody had torn up the paper and thrown it in the corner with trash. So, like working a jigsaw puzzle, she had put the scraps together, pasting them on the tissue paper of an old dress pattern so that she could read both sides. When Johnson entered the neat little cabin, the pasted-together paper was the first thing she showed him. Confusion overwhelmed the shy young Creek.

Diffidently, his eyes downcast, he peered at the paper, ashamed to tell her that he could not read. Whether what she showed him were hieroglyphics revealing how the ancient pyramids of Egypt were built, or the latest flyer for a sale of muslin undergarments at Cowley's Mercantile in Muskogee, he could not tell.

"Ah," he murmured in hesitant quietude, "I never had a chance to go to school—"

"Oh, I'm sorry." Her almost pretty face blushed the most exciting shade of sunrise pink Johnson had ever seen, and his dark skin tried to reciprocate. It succeeded only in turning hot, as usual. In reaching to take the tissue paper, her hand touched his. In contrast to his face, his hand went deathly cold. Her warm fingers against his felt pleasurably warm and stimulating. He felt his skin, over his whole body, turn rough and goosebumpy beneath his clothing.

She laid the paper on the table, his hand following hers down to the red-checkered tablecloth. Her long, tapered, and lovely finger followed the words, touching his hand all the while, as she read:

Into whose presence these may come; notifying Mr. (first name unknown) Coy and his (daughter or wife) that they are now established on properties pertinent to the (Creek) Nation of Indians, and that such presence is repugnant and undesirable to said Nation of Indians; they are ordered, immediately and forthwith, to remove themselves into the bounds of a state of the United States, or to other lands not pertaining to the Indian Territory, there to become resident. The bearers of this order are authorized to remove the subject (Coys), using such force as is necessary.

(Signed) *Sam'l Tsch-kote, Principal Chief, Creek Nation. Nathan Able, Agent to the Cherokees, Choctaws, Seminoles, Chickasaws, and Creeks.*

Johnson was mortified. He recalled now the astringent Coy, ripping this paper apart and throwing it down in anger. To think that he and Millar Stone had been the "bearers" of this torn-up document which Martha had so painstakingly restored, and that he might have to be one of the bearers of a similar eviction notice to her and her father . . .

Staring at her shining, angelic face, he tried to speak, knowing he was no good at lying, but his eyes again fell

away. He made his own fidgeting hands lie still then, re-
solving to tell her the truth, but when the words stammered
out of him they were not what he expected them to be at all.

"Maybe those Indian authorities won't be in an overpowering hurry to drive you out," he heard himself trying to reas-
sure her. He could not meet her eyes or even look at her face.
He was half relieved to hear the approach of her father's steps,
even knowing that the inquiry about the eviction of the Coys
would surely be more pressing now. Silan Lewis was apt to
demand details that might not have occurred to Martha.

Her father had heard Johnson's last, hopeful remark and
asked, "Where would I find this Samuel Tsch-kote, and the Indian agent, Mr. Able? I would like to go at once to see them.
We mean no harm here. But if we are not welcome we would
want to leave. In spite of the fact that we've been working
hard on improvements—"

Johnson saw the opening and leaped into the breech. "Improvements? Let's take a walk around the place. I'd like to see
what you've been doing."

Silan assented with pride. "Certainly. Let's do that." He
added to Martha, "We won't keep supper waiting, daughter."

As they walked out to the fields Johnson shamefacedly in-
jected another obfuscation, knowing it too was futile. There
was no way even to postpone, let alone prevent, what was sure
to be forthcoming, but he temporized, "I'm actually on my
way to Muskogee right now. I'll be seeing Mr. Able, the agent.
I'll try to say something to him about this. Maybe there's some
way something can be worked out." He paused for a long moment, then confessed, "I don't recollect whether I mentioned
this before, but I'm a Lighthorseman, a member of the Indian
police."

"Splendid!" Lewis exclaimed. "I'm told it is impolite, and
sometimes dangerous, to question a traveler like yourself in
this frontier country. Nevertheless, one is always curious. So
you are an official of the tribal government?"

"Just a common private," Johnson apologized. "That's as low as you can get, sort of like being a stray dog."

"I feel that we can get this cleared up," Lewis said optimistically. "Martha is more of a worrier, as her mother was, God rest her soul. She was always fearful, and lies buried, as she was afraid she would be, an innocent victim of a bullet in the internecine fighting that went on in Kansas while I was in Arkansas serving with General Blunt. A terrible, sad, and tragic time."

The conversation stopped. Johnson simply did not know what to say. They walked along in silence. He felt a swelling sense of sadness in his own chest. So much trouble for everybody, for Indian people and the whites, too, it seemed—a girl alone having to bury her mother, killed in a trouble she had had no part of—but he found himself staring with growing interest at the improvements Lewis and his slender daughter had made in the time that he had been up in the Cherokee country, then prowling south on the whiskey hunt.

The shanty man Coy's tumbled-down and decaying rail fences had been repaired. Crops had been put in—beans, corn, a potato patch. Some of the garden vegetables were beginning to sprout. There was even a small field of cotton Lewis was putting in.

"Just for a trial run," the settler assured his Lighthorse companion. "I don't know whether this is cotton country or not, and there was no one to ask, so we thought we would just try."

"I think your cotton may make it," Johnson speculated. "There is a Choctaw planter down on Red River who makes two crops most years, but it is likely too late for your corn. Here in the Creek country the corn crop has to be right well along by now. It's coming into summer and the corn has to have hot, humid weather to mature. Your stand is so young it will probably just burn up. Another moon and us Creeks will be dancing the busk." His voice trailed off.

He felt that he had been doing an incredible amount of talking, but Silan Lewis asked curiously, "Busk?"

"The green corn dance," Johnson finished lamely. Silan Lewis was evidently not enlightened, but Johnson said no more.

They turned around, retracing their way back to the cabin. Martha was nearly ready to set supper on, her face flushed and pink from working over the pots and pans racked among the hot coals of the fireplace. On Mr. Lewis's invitation, Johnson stepped outside to wash up at the basin beside the door. He used the big bar of yellow homemade soap with respectful care, certain that it was a product of Martha's long, lovely hands. He dried his face and hands on the clean towel beside the big white pitcher and washbasin, then took a comb that lay by the basin to his thick black hair.

As he stepped back into the cabin, he met Silan Lewis passing him on his way outside to perform his own ablutions. That left Johnson alone in the single room with the tall girl. Instantly, he felt very much alone with her—so strongly conscious of being alone with her that he sought something to say, but no words came out. The long, muscular Lighthorseman ducked his head in silent embarrassment, standing, he was certain, with gawky awkwardness. His eyes downcast, he felt like an ignorant lout, and this thought hung in his mind though he was unable even to put words to it.

"Sit down, please, Mr. Lott," she urged. Her voice had gentle musicality in it, like the tinkling of the small herders' bells Johnson had heard hanging from the fleecy white necks of the Chickasaw sheep flocks in Leander Dewey's country.

"We're still living on rabbit and squirrel stew," she said regretfully. "Seems like that's all we're likely to have until next winter when the weather gets cold enough to butcher a pig. Daddy intends to purchase a yearling heifer and a young bull and a litter of pigs. I'll be gathering the wild fruit that grows down by the river, so we will have sand plum preserves and possum grape jelly if you have a sweet tooth."

Looking at her as she moved about so gracefully, setting the steaming viands on the table, Johnson Lott knew he was ready to admit, if only to himself, that he did have a sweet tooth and that it was aching for the prospective maker of the jelly and preserves more than for any product her hands would ever make. The futility of such an emotion brought him again to the brink of sadness. Fleeting, dark thoughts once more besieged his spirit; for a simpleminded, know-nothing Indian like himself to aspire—

"But look!" she exclaimed, breaking into his dismal gloom. "We do have some wild honey. I found a bee tree. Daddy cut it down. Oh, we're not going to stay poor forever! We'll have chickens soon, too. We have one family of Indian neighbors, and when I went to see the lady she was kind enough to lend me a hen and a setting of eggs. I just have a feeling that we'll find people awfully friendly and nice here, once we begin to get acquainted."

After supper Martha stacked the dishes in a bucket, poured water over them, and said, "Those will have to wait for tomorrow. There is a more important thing to do tonight."

She got down brown wrapping paper and a thick-leaded pencil, and began to write. "Now these are the letters," she said. "A, B, C, D—say them after I do so you'll get the feeling of how they sound. They go together to make words. Here are some easy ones you already know. Cat, dog, cow, horse . . ." Before he had time to pull away, she was holding his hand in writing them, guiding his fingers in the cursive script. His hand was following hers, clumsily, then eagerly, and his heart pumped with excitement.

Time began passing unnoticed. Johnson was a timid but eager pupil and, presently, a happy and devoted pupil. To be working here with her, just to experience the sudden skyrocket sensations of her touch as she taught and explained and gently moved his fingers through the intricate patterns of penmanship was an incredible reward for willingness.

She said, "Why, I believe you could be an artist. Your hands have a talent for drawing. You learn the shapes of the letters so easily. Have you ever practiced drawing?"

He admitted that as long as he could remember he had drawn sketchy little pictures on mossy rocks and carved things from sandstone and pieces of wood as a time-occupying patience game to be played while waiting alongside hunting trails or just idling away time. "Most Indians learn to draw," he said. "It is the way the old folks keep the history, with pictures. Many draw much better than I can."

She looked around briefly, then set before him a small bundle of wild blooming thyme she had gathered. "Draw that," she suggested.

Johnson sketched it neatly on the paper. She took it, studied it carefully, then commented approvingly, "I don't know but what you should be teaching me."

She reached for the document she had jigsaw-puzzled together, to teach him some of the words it contained, Johnson supposed, and he wished she'd pick something else, seeing the sure and sad parting that paper augured for the future, but her father, who had been sitting and reading quietly before the fireplace, turned, yawning. "Isn't that enough teaching for tonight? It's almost midnight." He came, stretching and yawning, to lay his open book on the table. Johnson could not read any of it, but he could see that it contained pen drawings of many birds. Martha closed the book, ran her finger along the words of the title, and said, *Birds and Their Habitats.*" She pointed to the cover drawing. "Bald Eagle," she read.

Johnson had readily recognized it, but the word "bald" sent his thoughts off another way. Bald Bluejay, the bootlegger, he thought, and sadness swept over him. There were too many reminders of how short their association must be: Bluejay's threat to tell the agent about the Lewises; his own duty to tell the agent, now that Martha had begun to meet their neighbors. As isolated as they seemed back here in the dark hills, no night was black enough or long enough to hide them forever. Nathan Able, Tsch-kote, someone in authority, was bound to find them out soon. Johnson stood, retrieved his hat, and turned toward the door.

"Here, here," Lewis broke in. "Where are you going?" Martha was already pulling comforters from her trunk. "Yes," she declared, "you must stay the night. I'm going to make myself a pallet here on the floor. You will sleep in my bed."

Even the thought of laying his dark Indian skin down in a bed where she had slept threw him into flustration. The thought of sleeping in the same room with her threw him into a paralyzing modesty. His mouth opened, and closed. In dismay, knowing that he must give a little to prevent catastrophe, he hurriedly declared, "Of course. I'd planned to stay tonight. But I'll have to sleep outside. The first time a coyote howls, that horse of mine will break for tall timber and I'd be afoot. I've learned to sleep with one open eye on that cayuse!"

He hurried on outside and spread his blanket roll beneath the blackjack oaks beside the poles of the horse pen. After he had calmed down and dozed off, he slept with neither eye open, and his dreams did not concern Ceś-sē or coyotes, but the tall, almost skinny girl in the house who with such facility set his emotions to tumbling.

He got up early and spent another day with the Lewises, not because he wanted to, but because he could not leave. Steadily telling himself that the more time he spent with Martha Lewis the harder it was going to be when she had to go, Johnson milked the Jersey cow the Lewises had led in behind their high-sided wagon. After a breakfast of fresh milk and creamy oatmeal, he helped Silan clear away the brush and make secure from varmints the small post-oak chicken house Lewis had built to house his daughter's hen and her setting of eggs.

At midmorning he was summoned back inside the house for another session with the blunt lead pencil, the coarse brown paper, and the English alphabet. It did not seem like a childish task to him, but like a door swinging slowly open to reveal a provocative, delightful new world. He wished that he could instantly push it all the way open, and he jealously guarded every minute Martha offered him, for he knew those minutes were numbered. When they were gone, he could foresee no way to keep the door swinging open.

The afternoon was spent with all three of them in the field cultivating the newly planted corn crop, and Silan Lewis spoke of the joy of farming. "There is an altogether wholesome pleasure," he insisted, "in putting dry seed into the ground, then seeing the new life of green shoots appear and grow. If you get rain, that is. Farming is worrisome, too, because you can only bring from the ground what the earth and the rain, and in this part of the country the wind, will let you. I have seen a hot Kansas wind suck the earth dry of water, turn the ground to dust, and blow away your crop with it. That is grim and discouraging. But as long as you keep planting and working you have a chance."

It sounded to Johnson a good deal like the old Indian elders. They spoke with respect of the sun, the earth mother and her power to produce nourishing green growth, and the succulent flesh of the deer that fed on mother earth's bounty. They depended on prayer to circumvent the dark forces that sometimes came to stunt growth and destroy that bounty, impelling hungry people forth to make war and try to take by bloody force the productive lands of other people.

Johnson worked and thought, wielding his hoe. He took his sweaty turn driving the mules that pulled the cultivator, got dusty and dirty, thought about the forces that endangered Martha and her father, and worried about his duty to put those forces in motion. He had come here to think things through, and he had thought, but nothing was through. He knew he was only procrastinating, and if he didn't do his duty someone would do it for him. Toward sundown he unhitched the team of mules and took them down to the river to drink.

Martha and her father came along. Separating themselves along the brushy banks and willow overhangs of the clear stream, each of them took a private swim to rinse off the day's dust. Together, they returned to the cabin for warmed-over portions of last night's supper, and another evening of study, which Johnson figured would be his last, for he ended it with the announcement, "Tomorrow morning I have to ride on."

He spent a forlorn night secluded among the horse-pen blackjacks. After breakfast, a special one of flapjacks and honey, in his honor, Martha and her father accompanied him outside to see him off. It was a sad parting.

"I hope you'll be back soon." Martha smiled in an effort to make it seem cheerful.

Johnson nodded, willing to be hopeful, but without any idea of when, if ever, he might return. Neither Martha nor her father made any reference to his discussing with Nathan Able the chances of their staying in Creek country. Johnson was sure they did not mention it because they were confident he would do exactly what he said he would. He knew that, in spite of his promise, it was unlikely that he would ever open the subject with anyone.

Their confidence that he would be able to straighten out this business was due to take a mighty hard lick, Johnson thought sorrowfully, but he could find no way to tell them that right now. Knowing that he looked long-faced and down in the mouth, Johnson gave Ceś-sē's cinch a hard tug and stepped across the saddle.

"Don't be gone too long now," Martha urged eagerly. "You are doing so good both in reading and writing we mustn't postpone the next lesson too long."

With his hand lifting in a wordless salute, Johnson rode out of the yard. His head was empty of any constructive hope, or of any thought whatever. He let Ceś-sē pick his own slow pace down the narrow trace toward the Texas Road. There, something, not hopeful, but perhaps vaguely better than nothing at all, began glimmering. Johnson picked Ceś-sē up to an easy canter, then let him fall into a trot on down to the Katy railroad tracks and crossed them. Then, instead of turning north toward Muskogee, he rode south toward Tsch-kotah Town.

He might find old Chief Tsch-kote there. Tsch-kote it had been who had first recruited him into the Lighthorse. Like most Indians, the appointed chief of the Creeks had a way of sensing what was going on in your head, whatever outward appearance you might choose to counterfeit, and regardless of the words you chose to use.

Johnson was certain now that he would never be able to betray the presence of the Lewises in Creek country. Nor could he make any sensible explanation of his attraction to them. Worst, he had Bluejay to contend with. It was, the Lighthorseman knew, a far more serious dereliction of duty to remain silent about the bootlegger and his nefarious trade than to keep quiet about the Lewises. Whiskey had been the downfall of more Indians than any of the white man's diseases.

The Creek capitol was at Okmulgee, and Tsch-kote might be there. But except for the times when the House of Kings and the House of Warriors were in session, the chief seemed to prefer to spend a good deal of his time in his leathery-smelling law office in the old Indian town that was named in his honor. Johnson spurred up Ceś-sē and came riding into Tsch-kotah Town about noon.

He was delighted to observe that it was tradesday. The little frontier town was full of Indians. Tsch-kote was almost as sure to be here on a tradesday as he would have been if it had been a court day. The strange hope that had come percolating up in Johnson Lott's brain—that the chief might be able to see through him and somehow extract the truth from him in spite of his determination to hide it—freshened in the young Lighthorseman's mind. Maybe Tsch-kote might possibly even have some kind of a solution to propose for the Lewises.

Tsch-kotah Town had been built long before the railroad and so lay at right angles to it. Johnson turned west on the main street, *Meskólwv*-Oak, and rode directly to the hitch rail in front of a general store at the end of the block. Here he tied Ceś-sē and climbed the outside stairway to the law offices on the second floor of the frame building. *Sam'l Tsch-kote, Att'y-at-Law,* said the gold leaf lettering on the wavy glass panel of the upstairs door. Johnson felt a certain pride in recognizing the letters for the first time in his life and, because he knew the chief was an attorney-at-law, knowing what they said.

He entered the office confidently, without the formality of knocking. The waiting room was empty. In the large office to the left, Tsch-kote's clerk was working busily with his quill. To the right was Tsch-kote's own office. The chief was there, sitting before his big rolltop desk and also writing. Both men looked up.

The clerk arose to come out and inquire Johnson's business, but the chief had seen him too, recognized him, and beckoned, calling out in Muscogee, "Welcome, Private Lott. *Ascéyetv.*" Samuel Tsch-kote was small, a slight-bodied man compared to Johnson, whose build was rangy and athletic. His hair hung at shaggy, senatorial length below his stiff white shirt collar. A sparse, brushy moustache covered his upper lip, above a patch of gray goatee on the point of his chin.

He did not rise, but leaned back in his swivel chair to shake hands with the young Lighthorseman, softly and gently, in the Indian way, holding the light grasp while he inquired solicitously regarding Johnson's health. Before Johnson could reply, Tsch-kote was going on. "It is a fortunate circumstance that you should happen to be passing through here today. Choctaw Lighthorseman Buck Tom is here already, looking for you. He has gone out to purchase a few provisions and eat some dinner. He should be back right away."

Tsch-kote motioned toward his work. "I am writing to agent Nathan Able, requesting your help as soon as you can be made available. The Crazy Snake faction is becoming more and more unruly over the allotment matter. I believe you know those men better than anyone else we might send, and probably are, in fact, sympathetic to them. We must make overtures and try to reason with them before they break the peace completely. It is difficult to know how near that point they are—in spite of which I believe that Buck Tom's mission must take precedence right at this time."

Chief Tsch-kote shook his head. "The times are troublous, and it seems impossible to determine where to try to stamp out the fire first, but as soon as Tom comes back—good, here he is now. Hear what he has to say while I finish my letter to the agent."

CHAPTER 4

Johnson stared at the familiar, ugly features of Buck Tom, standing and grinning at him from the outer office waiting room. Chief Tsch-kote had returned to the writing of his letter. The Choctaw chuckled. *"Hērákoo!* Good! Come on out here. Let's get with it."

Johnson stepped quietly out through Tsch-kote's inner office door, closing it silently behind him. "Good? What's good? I come here to talk to my old boss. Now I have to listen to you before I can even say a word to him."

The broad-chested, heavy-bellied Choctaw's chuckling burbled noiselessly. "I figured you'd be around here sometime in your coming and going—to keep old man Tsch-kote told about where you were and what you were up to. So I come here."

Tsch-kote's clerk got up. He came with a mincing gait to close his own door and shut out their conversation. Johnson gave sardonic thought to the diligence of his own comings and goings to keep Tsch-kote informed of what he was up to. Buck sure has an exaggerated idea of my devotion to duty, he brooded. I haven't been here since snowfall last winter. He asked, "What do you want, *alikchi?*" Just looking at Buck's ugly, congenial, friendly countenance had Johnson almost grinning himself.

"Not *alikchi,*" Buck denied. "Not no witch doctor no more. Just private, same as like you. It's funny that the oldest Lighthorseman and the youngest one should both be privates. Don't you think?" Buck Tom chortled.

Johnson *was* grinning now. "Buck, you'd laugh if the Comanches had you tied to a post and their squaws were slicing your ribs out with scalping knives. You'd think they was trying to tickle you." He pointed his chin at Tsch-kote's closed door. "The chief didn't seem to think there was anything funny in your errand to fetch me."

"Maybe not," Buck conceded. "There is though. Kind of. Shelby McIntyre and Tim Gale are building a drift fence across the Arbuckle Mountains. That's kind of funny, ain't it? Building a drift fence forty miles long when Millar 'n Mutt 'n Lee 'n me 'n you are fixing to head down there with wire cutters in our saddlebags. Don't you see where that's got a humorous aspect?"

"All of a sudden, everybody is trying to string wire of some kind across the Indian country," Johnson groused. "What's funnier will be seeing them pussy-gutted ranchers doing a lick of real work."

"They've got six or eight cowhands helping 'em, along with Shelby's brother," Buck declared.

"That ought to be enough to keep the five of us busy." Johnson glanced back at Tsch-kote's door, which he had closed. There was no telling when the chief would open it. All right, Johnson alibied, he had come here and tried. Not very hard, he reluctantly admitted. But even if he had been eager to tell all he knew about Silan and Martha Lewis, along with Bluejay and his whiskey, he still wouldn't have been able to do it.

If I can't talk, I can't tell, Johnson reasoned. Tsch-kote hadn't let him get a word out. Better I just go along with this chore, he thought—Sam was mighty anxious to have me hear about it. He was preoccupied with Bus Vixico and his Crazy Snakes, and in no mood to listen. He's sure in no mood to see there's something on my mind I don't know how to talk about.

"All right, Buck," he asserted. "I reckon I'm as ready as I'll ever get. Let's go on our way."

As they walked down the outside stairway toward their horses, Buck amplified, "The McIntyres and Gale have been having trouble with their cattle drifting north during dry spells. They figure if a real drouth comes along this summer their stock might wind up in the states looking for grass and water."

"They can't fence the Indian Territory even if the country turns to desert and they are married to Chickasaw women," Johnson declared.

"The Chisholm Trail gives them some trouble, too," Buck rambled on. "Those Texas steer herds being hazed through our country to Kansas are looking for grass and water themselves. The herds are too big, and too frequent. They're keeping the pastures alongside the trail grazed right down to the roots. Some of Shelby's cows, and more of Gale's, I guess, seeing he's the furthest west, just ease in with a passing trail herd, get drove to Abilene and get sold there. Shelby and Gale figure that's no way to make money in the cow business."

"And to make money in the cow business is why they married Chickasaw women," Johnson said caustically.

The two men mounted to ride out of town. Johnson continued his diatribe on squaw men in general and the McIntyres in particular, concluding, "They're too fat and sassy."

"Wayne McIntyre ain't fat," Buck offered with a grin.

"The runt pig of the litter," Johnson scowled. They turned south, paralleling the railroad in leaving town.

"The funny thing," said Buck, ruminating, "is you hear about squaw men a-plenty, but there ain't no such thing as a buck woman. You reckon it's all because white men find our Indian girls so attractive or, like you say, because a Indian wife comes with a bonus—the right to use Indian land? You hardly ever hear of a white girl married to a Indian man. Are us bucks just bashful? Or do paleface girls find us vulgar and unelegant?"

In the railroad yards they were passing a train was making up. Freight cars backed and filled, the clash and rattle of couplings momentarily overriding their talk. Johnson listened to the clanging bell of the switch engine signaling ready as he watched the brakeman run along the top of the string of cattle cars, then stop and spin the cartop wheel to unlock the brakes. The train pulled forward, backed through another switch, and added another segment to its growing length. These distractions crowded into his head, dulling the chagrin caused by Buck's speculation. It seemed inevitable that Martha Lewis must find him unelegant, in spite of her cheery, friendly ways.

The chant of an auctioneer at the trade-barn cattle pens beside the tracks, soliciting bids for the cattle that would load the switching cars, filled his consciousness then, diverting thought from the hopelessness of the whole Lewis affair. It would not be long, he guessed, before the running of these trains would wipe out the need for cattle trails like the Chisholm. Trailing cattle was becoming unnecessary, and its passing would be hastened by fences like McIntyre and Gale's—provided that they were permitted to build them.

"Where are we supposed to meet Millar and the rest of the Lighthorse?" Johnson asked.

"Millar an' Mutt will be waiting for us at the big medicine springs just this side of the Arbuckles. That being Leander's country, he'll be over pussyfooting around the fence a-building, but he'll pick us all up when he figures out the best time an' place for us to go to work."

They rode on south, following the Texas Road the rest of the day, to camp that night on the headwaters of San Bois Creek. After unsaddling, Johnson pulled a pair of worn moccasins from his saddlebags to rest his feet from the long day in the tall black boots. Buck Tom broke open the packet of dry stores he had bought on Sam Tsch-kote's purchase order in Tsch-kotah. Then they fished long enough to catch a panful of bream.

The fish were frying briskly when the Choctaw asked, "You find anything on the big whiskey hunt?"

Johnson was startled out of the quiet reverie that had been holding him. "Uh. Why—some. I found some traces. How about you?"

"Choctaws ain't much on whiskey-making," Buck replied. "It's too easy for them to ford the Red River an' buy their hootch in Texas. They come faunching back across that river, riding hell for leather with a bottle in each boot—one to drink an' one to sell. I got in on some good chases. Them Choctaw boys took to expecting me, though. They'd be watching when they come back across the river and hit that bank like they was riding double with the devil. I'd take out after. Sometimes I caught up, but mostly they got away. They know holes to hide in, an' they pick their own time to make the run. Right about dusk when the light is bad, or before sunup, or in a rainstorm. Makes them hard to catch, but I caught a few and poured out their bottles. It's good sport. Beats chasing a real live mountain lion up a tree!"

In the saddle early the next morning, they turned off the Texas Road at McAlester's store, wandering across the hills in a more westerly direction, listening to the high wind that swept the grass flat in every coulee and draw, and making desultory talk to pass the day. Johnson pursued Buck's declaration that he was no longer an *alikchi,* wanting to know why.

"I met up with a real fine missionary couple over at Boggy Depot," Buck explained. "They convinced me there is a medicine stronger than any of us Choc *alikchis* ever had. So now I've taken to missionary preaching myself. If we ever get these Injun Territory malefactors halfway under control, I'm going to quit the Lighthorse an' turn full-time preacher."

"I've heard some of that preaching," Johnson admitted. "Been to an all-night gospel sing, too. Maybe they're all right. I still believe the square ground religion is the best way for Indians to go. That black drink purifies a man. The *Ispokogis* really know the way to the sun. There's nothing like a hard-fought ball game to get your meanness out and over with. Those old ways are the best ways, I think."

Buck Tom was willing to concur so far as admitting that he still enjoyed a good ball game. "My hands was just made to fit a pair of ball sticks. You get two big, strong teams really fighting to keep that ball and get it through the goalposts—it's like you say. It gets the meanness out and makes you feel good all over. Trouble is, too many gets hurt, and maybe somebody gets killed. That's against the missionaries' teachings."

Late in the afternoon the wind laid, dying away slowly; they caught the sulfurous odor of the medicine springs and began following down the travertine courses of Honey Creek, hunting for Millar and Mutt. They were not at the Buffalo Springs, where rock gas came bubbling up through the water like escaping balloons.

"Sometimes you can get those bubbles to burning," Buck attested, "if you hold a torch over the spring. They'll get to igniting each other, exploding with little pops like the barking of a town of prairie dogs."

"We've got no time for such foolishness now," Johnson replied.

They rode on down the fast-running stream, its water so laden with minerals that it had built up its own honeycombed rocks. They turned off to the Antelope Springs, where a great spout of white water gushed from the mouth of the rocks in a noisy torrent to rush downhill and join Honey Creek.

"No one here, either." Buck proclaimed the obvious.

So they rode on to the Stinking Springs. There, in the stench of the sulfurous geysers, they found Millar and Mutt loafing under the overhanging bluffs, taking the waters.

"You act like a pair of ailing, overage sachems," Buck Tom chided, grinning.

The pale, milky white water they drank from tin cups smelled like rotten eggs.

"It is sure good for what ails you," Millar said contentedly.

"Whether anything ails you or not," Mutt declared.

"Lee been heard from?" Johnson asked.

"He'll be waiting for us over at A'yo Falls." Millar Stone got up reluctantly. "It's hard to get going again. My joints set up."

"How long you all been here?" queried Johnson.

"Four or five days, I reckon." Captain Stone arched his back, stretching. "Just waiting for you two to show up."

Buck suggested, "You ought to be all freshed up and full of vim an' vinegar."

"It's not supposed to work that way," Mutt argued. "The longer you drink this foul-smelling stuff, the more relaxed you get. It makes you easy in your mind. You forget your worries and just get lazy."

Buck Tom chuckled. "And the drift fence gets longer."

"No use jumping out the fence makers while they got a three to one edge when you can get it cut down to two to one by waiting awhile," Millar said calmly.

"Just waiting for us two privates to come and do all the heavy work," Buck jested.

Johnson asked, "How did you find your families?"

Millar said, "Mine has got so big it ain't no trouble at all to find."

"My boys are getting tall and ornery," Mutt replied.

Millar picked up the saddle blanket he had been lying on and walked to throw it across his horse's back, followed by his single-cinch centerfire saddle. He mounted, drifting off due west to climb the high bluffs. The others followed leisurely. They did not reach the falls until the following morning, after a night's dry camp in the arid uplands beyond the medicine springs, among prickly pear and buckhorn cactus.

The roar of the mountain cascade increased as they approached from the downstream side. As the tumbling cataract with its streaming horsetails of falling water became visible through the slanting trunks of half-fallen trees in its flood basin, Lee Dewey came riding out of the timber to meet them.

"I've been watching you all morning from those travertine caves up yonder above the falls," he reported. "Makes a good place to hide out. A couple of days ago I could keep track of the fence builders by riding on up to the crest. They've worked on a considerable ways out of sight now. Must be getting near the west edge of the Arbuckles, almost into Comanche country."

"Maybe, if we wait another day or two," Millar suggested, "them wild Plains redskins will take care of this for us."

"They'll jump the fence builders if they get wind of them," Lee confirmed. "They might even rope a fence post or two and pull down a little fence. But heavy work gets old pretty quick to Comanche warriors. That'll be left for us. The fastest way for us to get that fence off Chickasaw land is to drop back to where they started, cut the barbed wire close on both sides of every fence post, and let it lay where it falls."

Mutt slid sidewise in his saddle. "Maybe we'll wind up fighting Comanches and ranchers at the same time." He sat with one leg hooked around his saddle horn.

"We're right in the middle of Scalp Alley," Lee said worriedly.

Buck Tom grinned. "The sooner we start the sooner we get through. Or maybeso we get our hair lifted. Then we'll be dead and out of all this trouble."

Mutt queried, "I still haven't seen any fence. Where does it start?"

"Clear back on the Washita. Beyond the Indian Meridian," Lee replied.

"Then we've already got near thirty miles of fence to lay down." Millar frowned. "Let's get started."

Their method of work was hopscotch, or leapfrog, working on foot, clipping the twin strands of barbed wire beside each post, then walking down the fence line past the four Lighthorsemen ahead to clip again. Loose herded along the fence row, their five horses were briskly enjoying their part of this particular duty. Hobbled, bunched together or spreading apart, the horses grazed, dallying to crop the rich limestone grass until one of the Lighthorsemen hazed them on down the fence row just to be sure they didn't fall too far behind.

Some ancient earthquake had heaved the limestone ledges

edgewise here. They slanted up out of the earth, erupting in serried rows a yard apart, oddly like the rows a planted crop of rocks might grow. Between them, the pasture was thick. The horses grazed to fit the patterns of the lush, pastern-high grass. As the afternoon passed, having grazed well all day, the horses became more frolicsome, in hobble-hopping chases around the mountain pasture. Mutt paused to stare at them playing like colts.

"For once," he said, "I do believe that ornery roan of mine has got his belly full of good grass."

He looked down at his hands. Blisters above and below the old calluses on his palms had puffed up and some of them had broken, exposing raw skin.

"They've got the best of it here," Millar said, glancing at the horses. "Let 'em run, I guess. They've fed themselves too full to run very far." He looked at Mutt's sore hands and shook his own arms wearily. "I'm finding some muscles I'd forgot I had."

They were not accustomed to such activity, and the gripping, cutting, and opening wire pliers in a steady clip-clack throughout the long day had strained hands, wrists, and forearm muscles to aching pain.

"Now look at that, will you?"

It was Johnson Lott's wry voice. He stood in the vanguard of the five Lighthorsemen, staring down the fence row ahead of them. Too preoccupied with broken, raw blisters and sore arms to observe much of anything beyond the place on the tough barbed wire where they were cutting, the others had failed to notice. Not far ahead of where they were working, the carcasses of dead coyotes hung from every fence post.

Patches of fur blew from the rotting flesh where buzzards had torn at them, and as the Lighthorsemen worked toward them the stink of death increased until it became overpowering. Gagging, Millar Stone undertook the duty of proceeding down the row, removing each coyote and putting it on the ground downwind. He came back, blanched and sick.

"Fourteen altogether," he said. "Unnecessary. Killing to be killing. Coyotes keep down the prairie dogs. When the horses of McIntyre and Gale's range riders begin stepping in prairie dog holes, these dead ones will have their revenge."

"The coyote is a medicine animal," Buck Tom said. "It is wise and tricky. The relatives of these dead ones, too, will find other ways of revenge."

Johnson felt entirely in accord with the Choctaw's *alikchi* prediction, but he recalled Buck's protestation that he was no longer *alikchi*. Turning to query, "I thought you said—" he was interrupted by the flat bark of a rifle shot and turned toward it in time to see Ceś-sē fall.

A scattering of other rifle shots following rapidly, almost simultaneously, brought down the other four horses. Only two fell motionless. The other three were wounded, kicking and neighing, trying to rise. Riders came in sight then, spurring up out of a cedar-edged coulee in the mountain pasture.

They came out of their concealment riding at a good clip, reining their mounts down the pathways between the up-slanted ledges of limestone. Only three carried rifles; fat Shelby McIntyre, his thin-bellied and sour brother Wayne, and Tim Gale. Some of the gaggle of cowhands riding along in the wake of their bosses had rifles in their saddle boots, and every visible rider wore a sidearm holstered at his hip, but the three leaders were the only ones with long-range armament drawn and pointed. They kept their rifles trained on the Lighthorsemen as they kept on coming.

Shelby McIntyre and Tim Gale were in the forefront. Johnson had seen them not long ago, on a Saturday, in Tishomingo. It was a busy sale day and they had been in town to do their trading. Johnson had been ordered down south to Tishomingo to help Lee Dewey regulate the mixed crowd. Both Shelby and Gale were pompous, big-gutted men; he remembered them trying to outdo each other in commanding attention, in demanding fealty from the hangers-on who surrounded them, rewarding their liege with heavy-voiced spiels meant to be serious advice, which prompted proper awe, or intended to amuse, which brought sycophantic laughter.

Gaunt Wayne McIntyre rode in now on Shelby's flank, his angry, deep-lined face bouncing beyond his brother's shoulder. The McIntyres did not look like they were related, let alone brothers; they were apparently able to tolerate beefy, over-bearing Tim Gale because greed obligated it if they were to control the vast spread of Chickasaw lands on which their two range outfits ran cattle.

The cowboys who had followed the trio up out of the coulee seemed to come along almost reluctantly. Johnson guessed they did not approve of shooting horses. However, they fol-lowed Gale's gestured orders to fan out and by the time they reached the fence the five Lighthorsemen were semi-sur-rounded against it. None of the riders spoke. The McIntyres and Gale surveyed the damage silently, then circled their horses and backed away to confer hotly, in inaudible, wrathful, hissing whispers.

Johnson knew that their fate was being settled in that con-fab of fury. The three rode back and Wayne McIntyre spoke. A good choice, Johnson decided. Either Shelby or Tim would inevitably have sounded as if they were bluffing. The ascetic, seething Wayne sounded dead serious.

"We'll give you the rest of the day to walk out of here alive," he said. "We'll be back before daylight. If you're still here, you'll be as dead as your horses."

Ceś-sē was not dead. Johnson could see that from where he stood. The mouse-colored gelding still kicked and struggled, trying to rise. The ranchers and their cowhand retinue sat there, as if to demonstrate to the Lighthorsemen that they could hold them hostage as long as the spirit moved them, to impress on the Indian policemen that they were at the ranchers' mercy.

Wayne McIntyre broke away then, Shelby and Gale spurred up to side him, and their hired hands followed. John-son counted. There were seven cowboys, ten men altogether.

He walked over to where Ceś-sē lay. The wounded gelding inhaled with a snort and got to its knees.

"You still want to play windbroke, don't you?" he said hoarsely.

The fencing crew was riding off in the direction opposite to that from which they had come. Johnson pulled his pistol, cocked it, pointing behind Ceś-sē's left ear, and shot. As soon as the horse lay still, he began rummaging in the saddlebag. The fencers, riding west along the drift fence at a fast gallop, were growing small against the horizon.

Millar came up to ask, "What are you doing?"

Johnson pulled out his moccasins. "I'm going to catch those scissorbills and kill them."

The Lighthorse captain walked around looking at the other horses, giving the death shot to the remaining two wounded, Dewey's Chickasaw horse and Buck Tom's tall bay. Both Lee and Buck still stood with Mutt beside the fence, looking off toward where the ranchers and their hands had disappeared. Stone turned to them, speaking loudly enough for all to hear.

"All right. Buck and I will head for the court down at Tishomingo. We're too old for running. Maybe we can get some kind of help organized. The rest of you are on your own. I'm not going to try to tell you what you ought not to do. I guess I'd rather you didn't kill anybody. Maybe you can pin them down somewhere. Anyway, keep track of them. It may be a week before we can get back up here."

Johnson had already taken off running. Dewey and Mutt swung in behind. There was no talk. Leaving the point to Johnson, Lee and Mutt followed single file. They headed out across the mountains, following the fence, into the sparse timber. There could be no doubt that the McIntyres, Gale, and their crew were headed for their line camp at the head of the fence. The high country timber was mostly cedar here, little higher than a horse and rider, and lightly scattered. It would not hinder them nor, if they caught up, conceal their quarry.

Johnson knew he could not run as fast as the horses had

been galloping when they had disappeared from sight. He suspected they would soon break that gallop in this rough terrain. He knew he could keep up this pace all night. He had often run for a day and a night together in a square ground ball game, at top speed and with utmost effort, capturing and hurling the ball with the *la crosse*-like sticks, simultaneously fighting off the attacks of opposing players and launching attacks of his own.

The Creek ball game demanded all-out effort, and he knew that Mutt and Lee, who played with Seminole and Chickasaw teams, were as hardened to ball play as he. Before dark Johnson could hear the fence crew ahead of him and could smell their horses' acrid sweat. The crew's horses had fallen into a walk. Johnson swung out to descend the Arbuckles' northern slope.

With Lee and Mutt close behind he ran for over an hour, bending gradually west again, then climbing back up toward the black horizon where the sun had set. A waxing moon rose behind them. Never easing their pace, they reached the fence and still ran on ahead, encountering a deep wash where heavy logs had been used to weigh the fence down, pulling its paralleled barbed wires down the bank to the bottom of the cut.

A heavy early summer rain had piled some debris against the big logs in the bottom of the run where Johnson, Mutt, and Lee crossed. They climbed to the far bank, and Johnson flattened himself behind the angling upthrusts of earthquake-slanted limestone. Mutt and Lee lay down beside him. All three were breathing deeply. None was panting or winded. Dewey started talking, softly, blandly, as if these thoughts he expressed were the musings of his own conscience, mildly spoken, and not meant to be persuasive.

"You're sure we passed them," Dewey said.

Johnson nodded.

"And now we're waiting for them." Dewey contemplated. "If we start shooting as they ride down into this gully, we can kill most of them. Maybe all of them. Then we become the ones running. From the white man's law." He waited awhile before finishing. "I expect the best we could expect would be that new scaffold over at Judge Parker's court in Fort Smith."

The desire to kill these jaybirds, and an irritating thought about another jaybird who was giving him trouble, passed through Johnson's mind, raising his ire. He knew what Dewey was up to.

"Now Wolcott Hobart, the Chickasaw judge at Tishomingo, is a man to give you a fair judgment," Dewey said.

"The McIntyres and Gale have the money and the power," Johnson protested, his blood still hot. "They'll just walk away from this."

"I've known Judge Hobart all my life," Dewey said in a calm monotone. "I expect he'll figure out a way to see these horse killers charged so they won't just walk away."

Mutt said, "Seminoles are never much for skipping a fight if there's a way to get into one. But Dewey's right."

The riders were coming. The sound of their horses' hoofs echoing hollowly on the thin limestone shale strengthened. The time for postponing shortened. A decision had to be made.

"Hell's fire, I'm just a private," Johnson protested in heat. "Mutt is a sergeant and you're a lieutenant. I've got no chance."

"No, now," Dewey soothed. "Millar said we were on our own on this. Whatever you decide I'll try to go along on."

Mutt said, "I know there's enough old-time Indian in you that you're going to do whatever you want to do. If you start shooting I anticipate I will too."

Johnson clenched his teeth. His thoughts spoke to Ceś-sē's departed spirit. You worthless mouse-colored horse, I aim to leave some blood as close as I can to where yours was let. To the approaching riders, as they came to the lip of the wash, he said, "Throw down your guns."

In the gathered dark, the pulled-up horses across the wash milled, silhouetted against the three-quarters moon behind them, and Johnson half imagined he could still sense in the hired cowhands their lingering distaste for killing horses. He kept his own heavy pistol well above the upthrust ledge behind which he crouched.

Beyond the wash, the sound of drawn and thrown-down guns began to clatter on the rocks. In the moonlight Johnson watched the three bosses, Wayne and Shelby McIntyre and Tim Gale, ease the rifles from their saddle scabbards and let them drop from their fingers to the ground. Gale then drew his revolver and tossed it away. So did the McIntyres.

All noise and no guts, like the Muskogee band's drum, Johnson thought. He slid down into the wash, crossed it, and began to gather up armament. Lee and Mutt stood up, holding a steady bead on the disarmed riders.

One of the abashed cowboys, in discomfiture, said, "You sure got the drop on us."

"Shut up," Shelby McIntyre spouted, and demanded of Johnson, "How the devil did you get clear around here?"

Johnson ignored him, calling out, "I think I've got all their guns."

Lee and Mutt came sliding down and crossed the wash. Using the riders' own lariats, they lashed their hands behind them and tied the horses in a column. Ejecting the ammunition from each weapon, stringing them on ropes by their trigger guards, and with three of the cowboys riding double to provide mounts for their Indian captors, the procession started the long night ride southeast toward Tishomingo.

They rode east along the drift fence to the point where the dead horses lay. Here they paused long enough in the light of the moon to gather saddles and gear from the stiffening carcasses of the fallen animals. All the McIntyre and Gale cowhands were now ordered to ride double, one of them with Wayne McIntyre.

This left a spare horse on which to pack the Lighthorsemen's gear. Awkwardly slung on its back were five saddles and the garland of trigger-guard-strung revolvers and rifles.

"Almost too much load for one horse," Dewey commented sensibly.

Johnson looked at the pair of overweight ranchers now dismounted and squatting miserably on the ground. "We sure can't make Shelby McIntyre and Tim Gale ride double on one horse."

Mutt Kiley concurred with a slow nod. "Sadistic cruelty to an animal. No one horse could carry them."

Shelby McIntyre spat on the ground.

The Lighthorsemen loaded the culprits again with some concern. With too many men and too few horses they began poking through the night. Stopping frequently to dismount, unload, and rest the laboring horses, they reached Mill Creek at a point some five miles south of the medicine springs where they had met to launch this fence-cutting mission. Turning south along Mill Creek, they followed it to its confluence with the Washita.

Upon reaching the Washita, sometime between three and four o'clock in the morning, they turned eastward toward Tishomingo. It was broad daylight by the time the Lighthorsemen herded their procession into the capital city settlement named for the Chickasaw chief who had explored this country and led his people west to it from Mississippi. It had taken Dewey, Johnson, and Mutt all night to travel a little more than thirty miles.

Across the dusty road from the square on which the capitol itself stood, a considerable crowd of mounted men appeared to be gathering and Millar Stone and Buck Tom could be seen riding among them. Proceeding on through the hock-deep dust of the road, Johnson, Mutt, and Lee herded their trail-weary captives up alongside the bunch of gathering men and halted there.

Millar Stone shoved his coonskin cap back on his head, thoroughly scratching through his hair with his fingers, and said, "By golly!"

Buck Tom laughed out loud. "We just about had a posse of these Chickasaws ready to come after you."

Mutt Kiley grinned. "We didn't want to keep you worrying."

Millar said, "I was afraid it would take us a week to get some kind of help organized here. These folks have come right through for us."

Dewey was riding about shaking hands with the possemen. He said amiably, "No use putting my Chickasaw brothers out. No use to make a long, hard ride when we could save you the trouble."

Millar addressed the gray-headed elder who rode the chunky, overage horse beside him. "Guess I'll have to apologize, Judge Hobart. We sure didn't need to roust you out of bed before daylight."

"That's all right, Captain Stone. I believe I recognize these gentlemen." He bowed his iron-gray head slightly. "Shelby, Tim, Wayne." He included the cowboys in his greeting then, and Johnson felt a forewarning that dulled itself on his own tiredness and was lost in a spurt of adrenalin at Judge Wolcott Hobart's next words. "Since we're already all assembled, we'll just hold the trial right here. Now."

"Right here" was a sprawling outdoor blacksmith shop in a grove of huge gum and hickory trees beside the dusty road. The early morning sun slanting under the trees sent long reaching shadows off to mingle with dusty sunlight along the road curving through the settlement. A scatter of split-log benches beneath the tall, thick-leafed trees that would soon provide pools of shade around them surrounded the coal-smoke-smelling forge and the anvil beside it.

This grove where Tishomingo's Chickasaws gathered to consider their problems was an outdoor town hall replete with racks of horseshoes. Watching the blacksmith forge the horseshoes red hot, shape them to fit, and cool them in the wooden tub of water nearby would fill any dull time when conversation lagged. The possemen were already dismounting, tying their horses to hitching racks around the grove, and seating themselves on the benches.

Shelby McIntyre protested, "Judge Hobart, this is a kangaroo court and you know it." He sat like a fat sack of shelled corn on his horse, the ropes tying his hands leading to rancher Tim Gale's bonds, and on to every other horse and rider. Being so secured had made escape during the long night ride a virtual impossibility.

"I'm the legally constituted judge of this district," Hobart stated. "As such I'm qualified to preside in any civil or criminal proceeding. This court is now in order." He picked up one of the farrier's hammers hanging near the forge, gave the anvil a ringing blow, and sat down on the bench beside it. "Lighthorsemen, help the prisoners to dismount."

Heavily, the bulbous McIntyre brother almost fell into Mutt's and Johnson's arms as they reached to help him off his horse. "I demand that we be permitted to secure counsel." He nodded his head up toward the capitol building on the hill across the dusty road, its native stone facade and ornamented wood dome catching the lifting sun's rays.

"No one will be in their offices yet," Hobart shrugged. "Who would you like?"

"Our business is handled by the firm of Crowley and Orff." Shelby included his brother Wayne and Tim Gale in a pompous but weary gesture.

"They will be summoned," Hobart agreed. "Meanwhile we'll get at the preliminaries of this matter. Lieutenant Dewey, see if you can locate Reid Crowley or Jacob Orff and ask them to come here."

A wagon driven by a Chickasaw farmer came pulling into town. He whoaed-up his team, sat for a moment surveying the gathering, then got down from his seat, tied up his team, and came to join the spectators. Whatever his reason for coming into town, it appeared less important than finding out what was going on. A wisp of odorous smoke curled up from the banked coals in the forge.

"Would one of you help me pull a couple of those empty benches up here?" the judge asked. "No use in you prisoners having to stand. We'll hear your side of this first."

Johnson helped, then leaned against a stanchion of the thick-poled frame used to secure a balky horse for shoeing. He listened to Wayne McIntyre testify. Shelby's gaunt brother, with asplike venom, told how he had been traveling toward the ranch headquarters near Dougherty. Riding in to order another load of barbed wire hauled out, he had, from the high pass south of Fort Arbuckle, seen the five Indians working along the fence with their wire cutters. He had turned back to the line camp to fetch his brother, Tim Gale, and the fencing crew to stop the fence cutting.

"Now when you returned to the scene of the action," Judge Hobart asked, "did you then ascertain that the men cutting the fence were Lighthorsemen carrying out their assigned duty?"

Wayne McIntyre sat glowering, his face sullen. Tim Gale cleared his throat on a rising note and struggled toward a more erect posture on the uncomfortable log bench. Johnson took a guess that this bulky but handsome man might be in part Indian, maybe as much as one-eighth Chickasaw.

Gale was getting ready to speak, but the judge, who could not himself have been of more than one-fourth Indian blood, interrupted. "You ranchers were surely aware," he suggested curiously, "that it is illegal to erect fence on Indian lands?"

A dominicker rooster and a parcel of chickens came wandering into the region of the smithy, the hens scratching in the dust and clucking contentedly. The rooster thrust out his breast and crowed a lusty greeting to the still-new day. Johnson moved to shoo them out, but they only scattered and regrouped noisily and went on scratching.

Judge Hobart raised a reassuring hand. "They're not disturbing this court, Private Lott," he said.

Johnson returned to stand against the shoeing frame, surveying the crowd of mostly full-bloods, but he could see among these possemen an admixture of every degree of part

Indian, with even a few pure whites other than the McIntyres thrown in.

Judge Hobart said, "I have seen you ranchers take increasing liberties with Indian law, expanding your lands, spreading your power. That your wife is Chickasaw, Shelby, does not justify such acts. Wayne, you are not an intermarried citizen and I am certain that you have no legal right to reside in the Chickasaw Nation. But since you are all here, Tim being part Chickasaw, Shelby intermarried, and Wayne sharing that patrimony, I assume all three of you feel that you have chosen to be Indians and that you are truly Chickasaws."

Shelby McIntyre immediately nodded enthusiastically, harrumphing with sham pride. Wayne nodded curtly. Tim Gale was determined to speak, his face suffused and choleric since Hobart had interrupted his first attempt. Gale burst out in fury, "My forebears were among the signers of the Treaty of Doaksville, which brought us here. They secured this land. I have the right to use it!"

"Yes," said Wolcott Hobart. "Since all three of you declare without hesitation or reservation that you are Chickasaw, you are subject to Chickasaw law. It is *prima facie* that you broke that law in building your fence. While officers were rectifying your depredation, you killed their horses. I sentence the three of you, Shelby, Wayne, and Tim, each to receive twenty-five lashes on the bare back with hickory withes. The horses that you and your men were riding are fine Chickasaw horses." He paused to look at the horses, counting them. "There are ten horses. I order them confiscated and given to the Lighthorsemen whose animals you shot. Third, last, the cowboys who were working with you are herewith sentenced to become a work gang which, under Chickasaw foremen, will remove and destroy all traces of the barbed-wire fence you were constructing."

CHAPTER 5

The withes were cut from the hickories of the grove, trimmed, and hardened in fire. Each Lighthorseman was to deliver five lashes to each of the McIntyres and Tim Gale. These three were stripped to the waist, then their hands were stretched above their heads and they were tied next to each other, to overhanging tree branches. Each of them had his feet lashed together and a heavy log was thrust between his boots. The weight of the logs so elongated their bodies that even Shelby McIntyre and Tim Gale were stretched thin. Wayne McIntyre looked as thin as a rake handle.

Johnson laid his switches on with a will, not savoring the howls of pain they elicited nor the blood they let, though it fulfilled his determination to let some as close as he could to where Ceś-sē's had been spilled. When he had finished, he walked to toss his fistful of withes into the fire that had hardened them.

He went on then toward the forge and anvil, pausing at the hitch rail where the ten Chickasaw horses were still tied. They were being admired by Buck Tom, who had drawn the short straw and been the first to deliver his five lashes to the two McIntyres and Gale.

Buck was gleeful. "These are some horses! Talk about forebears, I've heard that the ancestors of these horses were seen by John Adair himself, around 1775, when the Chickasaws still lived back in Mississippi and Alabama. Mister 'Give me liberty or give me death' Patrick Henry sent George Rogers Clark south to buy Chickasaw horses, and told him not to spare any expense in getting them. Clark said people were buying them up as fast as they saw them and the price was out of sight!"

Johnson observed, "I saw them bring thirteen men and their traps down out of thirty miles of mountains last night. I wouldn't expect any better proof than that of what they're worth."

"Any one of them is worth several like that crowbait you were riding," Buck chuckled.

I expect so, Johnson thought, but if that mouse-colored horse had his faults, so do I. And mine seem more serious to me. We got along good together.

Lee Dewey sauntered up. He stood placidly rubbing his unshaven cheeks as he told Johnson and Buck, "I finally found McIntyre and Gale's lawyers."

The pair of elderly and rheumatic attorneys were hurrying up, haltingly. What age had given them in wisdom it had subtracted in agility. They approached Judge Wolcott Hobart, who sat resting on the bench beside the anvil. The senior member of the firm, bent with age, cackled resonantly, "Judge Hobart, Counselor Orff and I wish to appeal your sentence to a higher court!"

Hobart glanced down in the grove, where Mutt Kiley was delivering the licks with his hickory withes.

"Why, lawyer Crowley," said the judge, "you're a little too late."

"Cut you some switches, Dewey," Buck chortled. "You're next."

Captain Millar Stone, who had drawn the long straw, was last. He finished the whipping at midmorning. Sweating, he peeled off his cap. "I've got to find me something to wear besides this coonskin," he declared. "These summer days are getting too hot."

They saddled up five of the Chickasaw horses and, leading the other five, rode to a general store where they bought the captain a leghorn straw planter's hat, then spent a leisurely three days on the return ride to Muskogee.

At the Union Agency, Nathan Able received them with ex-
clamation.

"By George, Millar!" he swore. "In that planter's hat you
look like a slaveholder."

"He is," Mutt said wryly. "There are four of us slaves."

Able surveyed the cavvy of horses ground-tied in the side
yard. "You certainly are the best-mounted slaves in the Territory."

"We drew to see which two belonged to who on the way
back up here," Millar Stone said. "Then we did a little horse
swapping and a good deal of horse training."

"I'll write Judge Hobart to thank him and the Chickasaws
for seeing to it that our Union Agency Lighthorsemen are so
well mounted," Able said. "You have considerable riding
ahead of you. The Crazy Snakes are gathering at Eufaula."

Millar suggested, "Johnson, why don't you and Buck take
five of those horses around and stable them while we try to
contrive some kind of scheme to frustrate your friend Buster
Vixico here?"

"Which five?"

"Well, that's hard to decide," Millar fussed. "It's a shame a
man can't ride two horses at a time."

They went out in the yard and took their time deciding.
Johnson and Buck led the spare horses off toward the Agency
outbuildings with Buck griping good-naturedly, "Let the old
man an' the kid do the flunky work. Us two privates. We are
the slaves, while the high mucky-muck officers sit back there
an' think."

The kitchen screen flung outward and Auntie Kerfetu threw
a bucket of slop water out across the backyard. She called
out, "Birds and beasts stay out of my way. I wouldn't want to
drown a blue jay!"

They walked on, Buck staring back at her curiously. "What
was that about?"

Johnson shook his head, feigning ignorance. "Who knows?"

he said loudly. "The older Auntie Kerfetu gets the stranger she seems."

They stabled the horses in clean stalls, leaving them dry hay to nibble, and as they returned across the yard Auntie thrust her head out the door again. "Dry stays a blue jay, day after day," she said. "It's the ducks that are wet. A wet blue jay is as strange as you can get!"

Buck shook his head. "Not as odd as a Creek cook who makes rhymes with her talk," he quipped.

Johnson walked on with downcast eyes, feeling very guilty.

They entered the office where Dewey was calmly relating the remainder of the fence-cutting fight for Nathan Able. Millar let him finish before he asked, "How much cain do you want us to raise down at Eufaula?"

"Just try to calm things down," Able urged. "The commission is still meeting in Washington."

"I think maybe the best way to do that," Millar suggested, "would be for us to scatter out from here. If we drift into Eufaula from different directions it may keep down the Snakes' suspicions that we've got a hair up our nose and are coming to make trouble."

"I think it is inevitable that the Congress will eventually insist on allotting the lands here," the agent speculated. "There are some things we are just powerless to prevent. I'm sorry to say that the West United Telegraph Company line has now been completed through the Creek Nation and they're building on toward Fort Sill. The company suit seeking damages for the telegraph poles cut down has been put on the federal court docket."

"If there's no hurry-up crisis on allotment we'll try to tell that to the Snake clan," Millar said. "Maybe they'll slow down a little. They are brave warriors and have a reputation for being foolhardy, which is how they got their name."

Johnson said, "They can sure be as crazy as snakes in a pitched battle."

Mutt grunted, "Or as crazy as Seminoles." His grunt did not seem to be one of disgust, but of pride.

They took their leave, Johnson steering clear of the kitchen as he departed. No use tangling anymore with Auntie Kerfetu. She knew as much about the strange bootlegger as Bluejay knew about the Lewises. Johnson began to feel that nobody was going to stay ignorant about anything, whether he told what he knew or kept his mouth shut.

It was a cinch he had to do something, or he might wind up being everybody's goat. But he had no idea what, and Johnson was determined that until he made up his own mind what to do he was not going to let Auntie Kerfetu or anybody else force him to do something he might later repent.

As if the Texas Road was somehow magnetized, and his new Chickasaw horse's shoes were made of especially ferrous metal, Johnson gravitated southward, headed for the Lewises' cabin. He arrived there barely before dark, making to Martha the shy admission, "I'm on my way to Eufaula. Thought I'd come by for another lesson."

Silan and Martha were delighted—especially Martha. They had already eaten, but she set out supper for him. Ambrosia fit for the palate of *Essaugeta Emissee,* it seemed to Johnson, for the garden was up enough to provide young turnip greens and fresh scallions to go with the homemade bread, leftover fried squirrel, and squirrel gravy.

Johnson ate hungrily, his appetite encouraged by the pleasant cadence of her voice and the movement of her slender form about the kitchen table. She talked steadily of mundane happenings during his absence. When she fell momentarily silent, Johnson, just to make conversation, filled in, "The green corn festival is only a few weeks away."

"What corn festival?" she asked pleasantly.

"The Green Corn Dance," he said. "It's the most important ceremonial the Creek people have. Once a year, in the summer time, the women use up all last year's corn, then clean house and light a new hearth fire from the sacred eternal fire our fathers brought from the old homelands. Then we make a feast with the new corn."

"Why, it sounds like a good time," she said.

"It's fun, but it's serious, too. You see, it's religious. The medicine doctor makes the black drink and they sweep the square ground clean for the new fire and singing and dancing . . ."

"Are you going?"

"Sure. I've never missed one since I was born."

"I'd like to go, too. Could you take me?"

The talk had been going so happily, in their shared joy at being together again, that Johnson made the promise lightly. "Sure. There probably won't be any other whites there," he cautioned.

"That wouldn't bother me. I know I'd be safe with you and I'll be quiet and stay out of the way."

Neither was what had been troubling Johnson, but he felt as if he had just been entrusted with the whole responsibility of the Creeks' tribal honor.

"Now let's get these dishes cleared away," she urged cheerfully, "and get down to the books."

The lesson was as delightful as ever, for Johnson emboldened himself to touch her hand at times when it was no accident. He purposely made a few letters less than accurately so her fingers would come to guide his to the kind of perfection they seemed to achieve so easily together.

In elation, his black boots hardly seeming to touch the yard, he finally made his way to spread his blankets under the blackjacks. After breakfast in the morning, they both came out together to see him off, with Silan commenting, "I see you've made a horse trade, and got the best end of it."

Johnson told the story behind the horse trade and sensed Martha's responding sympathy.

Silan Lewis empathized, "An old friend is never really replaced. Even in the welcoming of a new one."

"But I think I'm going to call this fine fellow Pos'ketv."

Johnson patted the blood-bay Chickasaw horse's arched neck. "In honor of the Busk—the Green Corn ceremony." He glanced shyly at Martha. "It means—like something new, rising out of old sorrow."

He forded the Ue-lau' kē and noticed that even the river was singing as Pos'ketv's hoofs splashed through the sparkling water, silvery in the morning sun.

Eufaula was a brand-new town. A venerable town previously located where the California Trail had once crossed the Texas Road, it had moved itself this far west to be reborn in the aura of hoped-for prosperity brought by the laying of the Katy tracks.

Johnson rode in through the humid summer heat of the July afternoon, patrolling the drowsy street, looking for a familiar face. Cicadas sang their summer song, each rising to its ratchety peak, then droning away to a steady whirr. It was a relaxing sound, fitting the idle emptiness of the nearly deserted town on this quiet midweek day.

There were few people about, and most of them were white, the new populace who had come here to build the town, now caught in the backwater of its stifling summer heat and humidity. Eufaula, a town too young, was suffering in a temperature that was no stimulus to bustling activity. The Lighthorseman at last saw a Creek man standing in the shade before the town's new red brick bank building.

Johnson knew the man was one of Buster Vixico's followers, but he could not recall his name. So he rode up to the bank, dismounted to leave his horse in the shade, and crossed the board sidewalk. It was windless and hot, even out of the sun. He exchanged no glance with the man leaning against the red brick facade, but walked on inside the bank and went up to the teller's cage.

The clerk inside, wearing a dark isinglass eyeshade, his sleeves rolled up, was sweating. His sweat assaulted Johnson's nostrils as acrid white-man sweat always did and he was aware of currents of odors in the faint draft of hot inside air circulating toward hotter air in the bright sunlight outside. The teller looked out at him dully, pausing in his indolent posting of figures in the ledger book spread open before him.

"Who's the fellow on the sidewalk?" Johnson asked quietly.

It seemed to rouse the bored clerk's ire—an Indian asking useless questions on a hot afternoon.

"I haven't looked. Do you expect me to . . ."

Johnson fished in his pocket and fetched out the badge he seldom used. It was a tarnished brass shield bearing the single word *Lighthorse* and a crudely stamped seal of the Creek Nation.

"Oh," said the teller.

"Look out and see," Johnson urged politely.

Every white employee in every enterprise in this new and ambitious little town was here by sufferance of the Creek Nation. Johnson knew they all were aware, and resentful, of the fact. Grudgingly cooperative, the clerk came out from behind his wicket and glanced through the glass front window.

"I'm not good at identifying Indians." The clerk returned to his ledger. "They seem similar. I think I've heard somebody call that fellow Spider something—Spider Wart?"

"Svpíke War'kē," Johnson corrected him. " 'Cut Off Together' in Creek."

The clerk shrugged with disinterest.

Johnson turned and walked out. On the sidewalk, he greeted the Indian in Muscogee Creek. There was no reply. Johnson was not so discourteous as to look directly at Svpíke. That would have been impolite. Instead, he looked off, abstractedly, across the sun-washed street and made another careful attempt at impersonal small talk.

The Lighthorseman got no response at all, so he went to stand, taciturn and separate, at the curb's edge. From somewhere down a side street he could hear the slow approach of a wagon, its dry board rattles, the squeak of a wheel needing grease, the clink of trace chains. The wagon came to the corner and turned, poking out in front of them.

A dispirited Creek woman sat dumpily on its seat. She tugged on the cracked leather reins in her hands, pulling a team of scrawny, spavined mules to a halt. Over the wagon's weather-bleached sideboards Johnson could see a sack of flour and an assortment of groceries scattered about the crack-warped wagon bed. Svpíke pushed himself off the bank's brick front, crossed the boardwalk unsteadily, and climbed into the back of the wagon over its slung-down tailgate. He had been drinking.

From his eye corners, Johnson watched the drunken War'kē, on his hands and knees, shove aside the litter of groceries to make a place for himself and sit down, heavily, cross-legged. The Indian woman flapped the reins, urging the team into motion. Johnson went down the boardwalk, stepped into the shade and across his Chickasaw horse's saddle, and fell in alongside the wagon. It would be, he figured, the simplest way to find Buster Vixico's Crazy Snake encampment.

Svpíke War'kē's woman drove directly to it. It was less than a mile south of Eufaula, in a bend of the Great Canadian. A parklike grove of huge burr oaks ran down the grassy flat to the river. Erected there, a motley bunch of wall tents, Sibley tents, carelessly built brush arbors, and camp clutter, made a hobo jungle of lazy disorder. As the wagon he had ridden out with pulled into camp, nothing much was moving.

The slight breeze of the hot afternoon moved the burr oak leaves gently and they spoke calmingly. Not even the scraggly cur dogs of the camp arose to bark or sniff at Johnson. The wagon stopped at a dirty tent not far away. Svpíke War'kē got out, stumbled toward the trunk of a tree and lay down in its shade, his head propped up against its rough bark. His woman began unloading the groceries.

Otherwise, there was no human activity. The few people visible were sleeping, or appearing to sleep, beneath the arbors. Some, dimly seen, lay supine under the rolled-up sides of the once-white tents. Johnson rode on into the camp. A dozing cur growled throatily when Pos'ketv's hoofs came too close. On a drooping clothesline, a dirty dish towel and a shirt stained with river mud lifted slightly in the faint wind.

The searching Lighthorseman found Bus Vixico's *gens* totem, a lightly fluttering pair of redwing blackbird's feathers attached to a dwarfed ear of blue Indian corn, swinging from the overhead of a loosely stretched tarpaulin. The rock oil with which the tarp had been waterproofed made a strong-smelling stench in the hot afternoon sun.

Under it, a windbreak of willow wands set in the earth concealed the sleeping area and presently young Bus Vixico stepped out of its overlap. Through the upright twigs, a shadow of movement suggested to Johnson that En-talb, Bus's subdued, browbeaten wife, was in there. Lighthorseman Johnson Lott dismounted.

Buster Vixico was near his own age, Johnson knew, and he knew that Vixico matched the translation of his name—Pitiless, or Remorseless, in Muscogee Creek. Johnson had hunted with him. Vixico stood bare-chested, thick-muscled, meaty-faced, phlegmatic. Around the waist of his soiled ducking pants he wore a belt made of the skin of a cottonmouth water moccasin, dark blue with flecks of brown. Its head hung from his belt, dull-eyed, dried open to expose its white mouth lining and poison fangs.

Vixico asked, "Have you finally decided to get right and join your own people?"

The Lighthorseman lifted his shoulders. He glanced around him. "Are all the Creeks here, Buster? It doesn't look like that big a camp. Where are the rest of the tents?" He wanted to ask "Where are the clean tents?" but he let that impression stay in his mind, unexpressed.

"Watch your tongue," Vixico cautioned. "Your loyalty drifts around like a stick floating in fast water."

Johnson tried to avoid sounding arbitrary. "All the Creeks don't agree with you, Buster."

"And you're one who don't agree."

"No. I think I agree with you. But the others, the ones who don't agree, they're Creek people, too."

"I don't know what you are." Buster looked him over in apathetic contempt. "I see your ribbon shirt and that long turkey feather in your big black hat, but those wore-out Lighthorse pants don't agree with the rest of your clothes."

"How?"

"They're white-man pants. And you run around in them doing what the white man wants you to."

Johnson said, "I guess—"

Vixico accused, "You're a white man's errand boy. What are you doing here?"

In growing chagrin, Johnson said somewhat evasively, "You say these are my people. I come to visit my people."

"Did you come to take off those pants, and join with us?"

"Nobody ever asked me to join the Crazy Snakes before, Buster," Johnson said sheepishly.

"I'm asking you now."

"I'll think about it," Johnson consented.

"Let me know." The torpid Vixico turned to reenter his willow enclosure, then stopped, staring off toward the camp's edge. Johnson's eyes followed. Mutt Kiley was riding into camp from the west. The Crazy Snake leader fixed his callous stare on Johnson. For a drawn-out moment his attention alternated between the two Lighthorsemen, then Vixico pushed aside the strip of canvas that hung down to cover the willow's overlap and went inside.

Now thoroughly embarrassed, but feeling there was hardly anything else to do, Johnson booted a stirrup, mounted, and rode to meet Mutt. The transparency of their mission, he felt, was fully exposed. Two Lighthorsemen riding into camp, singly or together, followed by three more, was not likely to be taken as a coincidence.

Mutt came in, unwrapping his turban. "Whew! This can't be any cooler than Millar's coonskin was. I'd go bareheaded if this heat wouldn't addle my brains." Beads of sweat stood out in his thick black hair.

He kneed his horse to a stop and Johnson, still disconcerted, reined up and sat in silence.

"What ails you?" Kiley asked.

"I just got a mighty strong invite to join up."

"With the Crazy Snakes?"

Johnson nodded.

"Hmmm," said Mutt. "Then here I come sashaying in. They'll see me—"

"I watched Vixico see you. If I was to pick up a rock and throw it, by the time it hits the ground every sleepy Snake in camp will know we're here, and have guessed why."

"So it *was* a mistake for me to come riding in here like this," Mutt admitted. "I guess I was worrying. My littlest boy was about half sick with the summer flu when I left home, and the other two are bound to catch it. But Millar's idea that we could come riding in here as innocent as if we were coming to a sociable stomp dance never did seem sensible to me. It's like five coyotes trying to cozy up to the sheepherder's dogs."

"This is a sullen bunch, out of humor with everybody, including themselves." Johnson fretted, "And I don't know but what they are right."

Mutt looked around at the tall, spreading burr oaks, the sun-washed grass, the sheen of the broad river and its wide brown sandbars. "They sure picked a pretty place to camp. It's hard to see how anybody could stay sullen here."

"They figure the moguls in Washington are going to take it away from them. This good, sandy bottomland will wind up part of some white man's farm."

"I expect so," Mutt assented. "Let's get out of this sun. It's frying my scalp lock."

They rode out and away from the camp. Mutt thought they might try to intercept the arrival of the others. "Let's try for Millar first," he suggested. "He'll surely come down the old Spanish Trail through those Cherokee hogbacks north of

Webbers Falls. He'll turn west at Briartown and come up the river."

"If he comes up the river we can hardly miss him," Johnson said.

From the bluffs downriver and above the Crazy Snake camp they set up the watch, and both of them were right. Millar was only a speck making his way through the willow bottoms when they first spotted him. The sun was dipping into the river woodlands to the west as they rode scrambling down the bluff to head him off.

Millar asked questions, heard out their answers noncommittally, then observed, "Indians can sure get antagonistic to Indians. I'd hoped we could at least talk. I didn't anticipate that they'd be altogether stiff-legged and chary."

Mutt brushed a swarm of summer gnats away from his horse's ears, reflecting thoughtfully, "Those tents even smell hostile."

Millar queried, "This Vixico has virtually told Johnson to throw in with them or get plumb out of the country, ain't he?"

"I don't think they'll let me stay overnight unless I'm committed to join them," Johnson concluded.

"We won't try then," Millar decided. "No use starting something we're sure we can't finish. We'll lay out in the brush and try to catch Dewey and Tom when they come up from the south."

With Millar leading off, they proceeded upstream a safe distance, they hoped, south of the camp, and set out a watch over the semicircular area surrounded on three sides by the swinging big bend of the Canadian. The oak park where the tents were clustered was at first quiet, but as night fell and the day cooled, it began to come to life.

From his post of concealment in a thick stand of salt cedar and willow scrub, Johnson could hear the hullabaloo intensify. They've got some whiskey, he thought. By full dark there was drumming, singing, and shouting, both male and female. As the night progressed it became the kind of hell raising he'd heard issuing from Muskogee's bawdy houses when the railroad was building through.

Johnson figured that, for sure, they had plenty of whiskey. Women laughed and screamed shrilly, interrupted by men's hoarse cries and some gunfire. After almost a whole night of it, toward morning, the wildness of the carousing began to taper off. Millar Stone and Buck Tom came sneaking up on him through the underbrush.

Buck chuckled. "That is some shivaree they've been having over there."

"Tom came in while they was going strong," Millar whispered. "I figured we might as well let 'em get it over with. It'll be daylight in another hour. We'll make our move before they get good and awake and their hangovers wear off. Let's go find Mutt."

They headed for Mutt's position on the perimeter of the semicircle, and saw the shadowy forms of two horses. Millar, Buck, and Johnson wriggled up to where Mutt had stationed himself, and found Dewey lying beside him.

"How'd you find us?" Millar asked the Chickasaw Lighthorseman.

"No strain," Dewey said laconically. "You all crawling around through the brush sounds like a herd of wild hogs stampeding."

Johnson knew that the infinitesimal sounds they had been making would have been perceptible only to Dewey's acute ears.

Buck Tom laughed. "You didn't have no noise at all to home in on like I did."

The camp off yonder was quiet now.

With the first roseate pink rimming the eastern sky, they mounted up. "Stay close to me, Johnson," Millar urged. "I'm going to make my pronouncement in English, but there'll be a-plenty Snakes in that camp that don't understand English. My Cherokee won't be no help. Cherokee is as different from their Muscogee Creek talk as Irish is from a Chinaman's jabber."

"The rest of us might need some of Johnson's interpreting," Mutt cautioned. "Us Seminoles, Choctaws and Chickasaws are supposed to speak Muscogee too. But we've lived apart so long our dialects don't match. We say the same words so different I can't understand what these backwoods Creeks say."

Spread wide apart, like a line of foragers, they approached the Crazy Snake camp. It lay smothered in dawn silence. Thick quiet hung about the tents like a miasma. At the edge of camp, Millar held up his hand. He cleared his throat.

He shouted, "Now, you folks, this is the Indian police. We don't want no trouble, but we're going to make a scout through this camp. We expect all of you to come outside your tents. But don't lay hands on no weapons or it could get mighty bloody. A lot of people could get hurt."

Patiently, routinely, they began to search. Millar motioned for Johnson to follow as they entered the first tent. Dewey, Buck, and Mutt remained mounted outside, watching to see that no Indian took off for the timber to hide his whiskey. Their job, at first, was easy. Still drunken men and women, insensible from last night's orgy, had hardly been aroused by Millar's warning shout.

They slept comatose, snoring, dressed or naked, as they had fallen asleep. Millar and Johnson prowled through bedding, cast-off clothes, satchels and bags, confiscating the whiskey they found. They passed bottles, jars, and jugs—full, part full, or empty—to the Lighthorsemen outside. When told that the saddlebags of all five horses were full, Millar dumped groceries from a burlap gunnysack in one tent and they began filling it.

"We're going to get most of it," Millar grunted quietly. "There's not much place to hide anything in a tent. Especially when you're too drunk to hide it."

The sleepy Creeks were beginning to rouse. A growing undercurrent of angry talk around the camp reminded Johnson of the threatening buzz around a bee tree in the summertime.

As the Lighthorsemen worked their way from tent to tent toward the upper edge of the camp, the Crazy Snakes, with their women and children, began emerging to gather in clots and bunches under the oaks and in the hotly rising sun. They were an indigent-looking outfit.

Men, women, and kids were dressed in seedy, hand-me-down clothes; they were plainly impoverished and destitute. In desperation, like aggravated bees, they began to swarm. Even Buster Vixico had slept through the search of his willow compound, but as the searching Lighthorsemen approached the last tents at the far edge of camp, Vixico appeared. He struck out, walking from group to group.

Millar and Johnson searched the last tent with its occupants glaring at them as Millar advised them to act carefully and to get dressed. Seething tension was ripening into aggressive hostility. Johnson followed Millar outside the final tent to see the three Lighthorsemen there standing guard over the full gunnysack with drawn pistols.

"Haul it down there by the river," Millar said grimly.

He mounted up and Johnson followed suit.

Dewey lifted his braided thong catch rope from his saddle horn, looped and tied it around the mouth of the gunnysack, and rode off dragging it. Together, they reached the rocks along the riverbank and undertook the pouring out of the whiskey on the ground. As it gurgled and splashed and the air became redolent with the smell of it the gathering Crazy Snakes crowded around them.

Dewey asked, "What about the empties?"

"Break them on the rocks," Millar said. "If we don't they'll take them somewhere and fill them up again. I sure wish we knew where all this whiskey come from."

Johnson, suspecting with near certainty where it had come from, felt fresh and overwhelming guilt, but this was no time to unburden himself. The Crazy Snakes were pressing in close. The smell of them and their dirty, vomit-stained clothes made a stench. Buster Vixico came edging through the smoldering crowd of down-and-out, rebellious Indians.

"You bring plenty company when you come to visit," he charged, not angrily, but bitter.

Millar was blunt. "You folks look to me like you could find something better to do with your time than to lay around getting drunk."

Vixico did not turn his attention away from Johnson. "I guess you decided not to join us." His voice was mordant, obdurate.

He did not appear to be armed. Johnson flicked his glance through the swelling crowd and saw no firearms.

"I haven't had time to think it out, Buster," he said thinly. "I still agree with you about the allotment, but my mind isn't made up what I ought to do about it."

Buck Tom said whimsically, devilishly, "He's been too busy working."

No one smiled or laughed.

Buster Vixico accused, "All of you come to steal."

"Pouring out contraband whiskey ain't stealing," Millar declared stubbornly. "If there was a jail in the Creek Nation big enough, we ought to pour you all into it."

"Whiskey helps us forget," Vixico replied sourly.

"How you going to forget all the headaches you got this morning?" Millar Stone demanded. "You ought to be out working."

"We used to have a big field, right there across the river," Vixico said. "It was six miles wide and almost ten miles long. We all worked in it together. Nobody cultivated just his own piece of it. We all started at one end and worked to the other. We still remember the songs that we sang while we did that, and everyone, even the chiefs, worked side by side. There wasn't a shirker among us."

"Why aren't you still doing it?" asked the Lighthorse captain.

"Why should we, when the whites are going to take it away

from us? We don't want any treaty that would make each of us work his own little piece of land and give the rest to the white settlers. That is what those men in Washington want us to do. We won't take allotment. We like the old way. We want to talk straight and work the land in common as it has always been."

"Well, I think that is all right," Millar said. "You spoke your mind, Buster, and I'll speak mine. I'm not for allotment either. You'll find mighty few Indians that are. But any kind of working is better than laying around swilling booze all night like you folks are here."

Hardly seeming to hear him, Vixico clung to the past as he remembered it. "Everybody worked except the sick, the widows, and orphans. For them we built houses and took care of them."

"You're making worse troubles," Millar accused, "than the white man makes for you. Helling around, getting drunk and chasing somebody else's woman like some of you were last night don't make things better. I heard some shooting over here. Pretty soon you'll be shooting each other—"

"Pretty soon we'll be shooting white men."

"That'll be a big help. You think Indians haven't tried that already?" Millar asked ironically.

"Right now we're having some fun," Vixico insisted, "the way the whites taught us to do. Drinking some of their whiskey. But we're making some other plans, too. We got some of the whites' guns, along with their whiskey. We'll get more of both. I make a personal vow to kill any white man who does anything to bring on allotment."

He turned to motion his followers away, waving them back toward the tents. As the Crazy Snakes dispersed, the Lighthorsemen kept breaking jugs, bottles, jars, and presently found themselves working alone. With the Snakes back in their tents the campsite looked as deserted as it had when Johnson had arrived the day before. Although no one was visible it seemed to him that the atmosphere of hostility hung in the air almost

as palpably as when the Crazy Snakes had pressed close
around them.

Indeterminately, Millar Stone kicked broken glass down the
bank into the river and said gloomily, "Maybe they'll stay
sober for a while anyway. As long as they stay in camp and
keep the peace there isn't much else we can do. There sure
isn't any jail around here that'll hold 'em. Dewey, you an' Tom
stick around and keep an eye on 'em, while the rest of us ride
back to Muskogee and talk it over with Mr. Able."

On the road to the Agency, Johnson kept thinking about
Buster's argument recalling the old days. It was persuasive and
nostalgic, but Buster was forgetting, or leaving out, the taskmaster—the *sátku pucáse*. It was his duty to divide the work
evenly, and Johnson had watched whippings with switches,
like those the McIntyres and Gale had received, administered
to both Creek men and women who had been summoned to
work but did not come.

He remembered seeing fields occupied only by women while
the men were off to ball plays or gone hunting. He knew the
tribal taskmaster sometimes confiscated the horses or guns of
those who were dilatory in performing their share of the work.
He remembered a Tuckabatchee taskmaster who had not always been fair in choosing whose horses or guns he confiscated.

Johnson still liked the old ways; they seemed familiar and
comfortable. He liked to remember, especially, the good
things. It was not easy to remember everything, he thought,
but it did not make much sense to leave out all the bad things,
as Buster did. They had to be thought about along with the
good in deciding what to do.

The three Lighthorsemen stopped at Ulfilas Racket Store.
It stood on the edge of Muskogee, ready to outfit settlers traveling down the Texas Road. From its sutler's stock of U.S. army
surplus, Mutt purchased a Union army officer's forage cap, to
replace the turban he had quit wearing in Eufaula. Then they

headed on up toward Agency Hill. As they approached the tall-columned white house's veranda Nathan Able must have heard them coming, for he appeared in his office door.

He watched them expectantly, and came walking out to meet them, saying, "Private Lott, are Captain Stone and Sergeant Kiley still on the same side? It would seem that with the captain wearing a southern plantation hat and the sergeant in a Union officer's cap, one of them ought to have the other in custody." He smiled at his own joke while managing to look as worried as usual in spite of the smile.

Millar was tying his horse to the extended arm of the front yard's small iron statue of a black stableboy. "Mr. Able," he said, "the Snakes are sure laying off to make trouble." As they proceeded on into the office he related what had taken place at Eufaula.

They seated themselves, the agent suggesting, "We will have to try to patrol the Green Corn Dance where the Crazy Snakes participate, and any large, mixed gatherings of people like the Muskogee Indian Fair. In the meantime, I'll make an effort to distract Vixico and his crowd. The time is ripe for the five of you to travel over into the plains and see if you cannot contact influential members of the Kiowa and Comanche tribes. Those wild Indians are stealing cattle and horses from the Chickasaws and making Scalp Alley a nightmare."

"Five Lighthorsemen are going to have a hard time pacifying two tribes of horse Indians, Mr. Able," Millar protested.

"No, no. Avoid trouble," cautioned the agent. "Just invite them to attend the Indian Fair in August. Perhaps if we could host them as guests we could show them a good time and make a friendly alliance that would cut down this thievery and bloodshed. Tell them we'll provide all the food. Just bring themselves, their tepees, and any beadwork or crafts they'd like to sell."

"We left Dewey and Tom in Eufaula to watch the Snakes," Millar reported.

"Pick them up as you go back through," Able recommended. "I'll try to take care of the Snakes while you're gone. I feel that all of you should go on this mission—a representative of each of the Five Civilized Tribes, you see. I'll ask Auntie Kerfetu to keep an ear out for activity among the Snakes." He smiled widely and easily for the first time during the interview. "She's getting to be my intelligence agent. Oh my, the things she tells me after there's been a delegation here from one of the tribes and she's entertained their wives in the kitchen!" He shook his head amazedly.

A shaky feeling quivered insecurely in Johnson as he wondered when she'd get around to telling the agent about bootleggers, blue jays, and a settler family named Lewis.

Nathan Able said, "After you finish there you might as well try to go home for a short visit with your families. I might go down to Eufaula for a visit with the Crazy Snakes myself," he mused.

CHAPTER 6

Johnson rode south between Millar, wearing his new, broad-brimmed planter's hat, and Mutt, with the black-visored cloth forage cap shoved on the back of his head. His own black sombrero made a broad shade in the hot July sun, but beneath the sombrero's high, feather-bedecked crown Johnson's brain was boiling.

He wondered about the Lewises. Had anybody disturbed them? Was there a way he had not thought of for them to be notified that they were going to have to move on? He could not think of anything. Such a notice would have to be carried by himself or one of the Agency's other four Lighthorsemen.

Surely Mr. Able still knew nothing. Otherwise he would have mentioned it. If he found out, he would not carry such a notice alone—but he was talking about visiting the Crazy Snakes alone. Johnson decided there was only one way to satisfy his mind for this present moment. When they reached the point twelve miles south of Muskogee where the faint trace turned off the Texas Road to the Lewises' cabin, Johnson told his friends he had a matter to take care of.

He turned off the trail without telling them where he was going or what he intended to do, and rode away. He left them halted and staring at his long, straight back in surprised curiosity. When he reached the Lewis cabin he called out, "Ma'am —Martha?" It gave him an exquisitely private sense of disquiet just to call out her name.

She came outdoors at once. "Oh, Johnson. I'm so pleased to see you! You've come to do some more reading and writing."

"No, Miss—Martha." Again that supremely hedonistic thrill from only mentioning her name.

"Then you've come to celebrate Independence Day with us."

"Independence Day?"

"It's the Fourth of July," she reminded him.

Johnson knew that it was the fourth day of July, which meant, in this particular year, that it would be fifteen more days until the Green Corn Dance.

"Our independence from the British tyrant," she urged. "The Declaration of Independence."

He stepped down from his horse, still puzzled. She was talking of something he had never heard of and did not have time to inquire about.

"I guess us Indians don't have much independence to celebrate," he apologized shyly. "And I've got to ride on."

Martha had made no mention of having received any notification to move. She seemed as brightly cheerful as ever. Surely she had heard nothing to alarm her, nor anything to make her sorrowful. He decided not to take a chance of alarming her or of making her sad himself.

Johnson was suddenly glad that he had not started out by asking if they had received any kind of official notices, for that would have made him become the bearer of news he now knew he never wanted this girl to hear. On the crest of his relief, of knowing the secret was still a secret, followed by an equally sudden dread of the day when it might not be, he reached and took hold of her hands. She was as astonished as he was.

"I'm going off on a Lighthorse errand," he said.

"Daddy is just down in the field. Won't you have time to see him before you leave?"

"No." He clung to her hands and she made no effort to remove them. "We'll be gone for a while," he said, "but I had to come by and tell you that, if something doesn't go wrong,

I'll be back to take you to the Green Corn Dance just like I promised."

The yearning to have her in his arms, pulled close against him, became an awesome thing to Johnson Lott—a void that, as nature moves to fill a vacuum, longed to be filled. He stood strong against it, clinging to her hands and suffering this futile yet desperate longing.

Dropping her hands, he booted a stirrup, seized the saddle horn for a hurried swing aboard Pos'ketv, and spurred the big Chickasaw horse out of the yard. He was tense and shaking. That he could have been so bold made him quiver. That he had so abruptly left *her* staring at his back appalled him. How she might feel after being so accosted by a dark-skinned Indian he could not fathom.

Johnson drove Pos'ketv running, back to the Texas Road, where he turned toward Eufaula and dropped into a steady gallop, hurrying to catch up. Within two hours he had done so.

Saying nothing, he fell in, riding again between Millar and Mutt. He did not speak and neither of them asked him where he had been. They rode on without invading his silence. He still felt shaken, dreading the questions that must inevitably come sometime, but thankful that he was not having to try to think up answers to those questions now.

Beyond Eufaula, they went straight on to the Snake camp and picked up Dewey and Buck Tom. Both of them were bored with loafing around the lethargic encampment. The loss of their whiskey in the confrontation with the Lighthorsemen seemed to have left the Snakes without a sense of direction.

"They lay around and sleep in the shade," Dewey said, "or get together in somebody's tent to smoke and talk."

"We don't get invited in." Buck Tom grinned benignly. "Sometimes they hitch up a wagon or two and poke into town. Dewey or me stays here an' the other'n goes along. If they've got ahold of any whiskey, they ain't drinking it."

Departing due west, the Lighthorsemen traveled for five

days along the California Trail laid down by Forty-niners dreaming of riches at the far-off California Golconda beside Sutter's Mill. At the landmark the goldseekers had called Rock Mary they turned south, trotting their horses toward the Wichita Mountains and Chief Stumbling Bear Pass.

No one had yet asked Johnson where he had gone on his unexplained lone foray below Muskogee. He decided that either his friends were not curious, or they trusted him. If it were the latter, he wished that he could have deserved it. They rode patiently toward the Wichita Mountains, looming there before them, multitudinous, many-shaped, rocky, and shimmering with heat waves.

Low and blue against the horizon, the mountains gradually assumed a subdued red hue, losing their soft appearance and becoming hard shapes of red granite. Boulders, cliffs, and shards of rock were relieved only by twisted, gray-green scrub oaks. Blue-green and bright yellow lichens dotted the mammoth granite boulders.

Halfway through Stumbling Bear Pass, in the far, far distance, Johnson could see what appeared to be a dead tree stub thrusting straight up above the granite rubble. The afternoon was wearing on before Johnson decided, for no reason that he could explain, that the dead tree stub was a man. He said so to his four companions.

Millar Stone surprised him by saying, "It sure ain't never moved, but that's what I make it out to be."

Lee Dewey drawled complacently, "This is as good a time as any to test the air."

They turned off across a broad, grassy meadow and rode toward the distant figure.

"He's wrapped his blanket from his head to his heels," Buck said. "That's why he looks so straight up and down."

"Pretty hot day to be wrapped in a blanket," Mutt suggested.

"Not up where he is," said Millar.

Before they could arrive within hailing distance of it, the

figure disappeared. It was there one minute. The next it was not.

"Anybody see him move off?" Millar asked.

No one had.

Millar grunted.

They reached the foothills and kept on riding into the scrubby, tangled blackjack timber. Somewhere ahead of them, an owl hooted.

"Johnson," Millar asked wryly, "was there a owl sitting on that tree stub we saw?"

Buck Tom's broad mouth spread in a grin so wide it wrinkled his flat, spatulate nose.

Dewey said, "It's too early for an owl to be sitting on anything out in sight."

Mutt said, "No Seminole owl would have such bad manners as to hoot before dusk, or more likely, full dark."

"Then that sure enough must be a Kiowa or a Comanche owl," Buck conjectured.

An answering owl hoot came from behind them, closing off the route by which they had entered the timber. They reined their horses to a halt.

"This," Mutt said, "may be where we find out whose medicine is the strongest."

Millar shook his head. "It just ain't no atmosphere in which to invite somebody to come to a fair. Nobody ever has medicine strong enough to make peace when the squaws are mourning over dead warriors."

"You mean our little army might hurt somebody?" Buck Tom queried genially.

"Some army we got," Millar snorted. "One sorry captain, a lieutenant, a sergeant, and two privates."

Off in the sham twilight of the timber, a coyote howled.

"Was that real?" Dewey asked.

"No," said Johnson.

Ironically, Mutt said, "This timber is just full of wildlife."

There was no banter in Millar's comment. "They got us

pinned down." He called the spade a spade. "We better make camp and try to look as peaceable as possible."

Through the thickly entangled treetops, Johnson was watching the sun settle behind the vapor of a fleecy cumulus cloud. "We won't get to see the sun set this evening."

"You've probably seen your last sunset, boy," Buck chuckled, but nobody else laughed.

They made a dry camp, not far from water, for they could hear it running rapidly. A mountain spring was somewhere near, but Millar suggested this was no time to get separated, so no one volunteered to go. It was getting dark fast in the brier-tangled motte of blackjacks.

After a while of chewing on a salty strip of jerky, Mutt offered, "We could all go."

"That's what they expect us to do." Buck chuckled. "Someone would sure have the honor of losing his hair by a pretty little pool right here in the middle of Scalp Alley. Put up that salty meat and suck on your teeth."

As darkness fell they built a big fire to demonstrate their courage. They encircled it, all sitting around it, facing outward, rifles in their hands, sidearms drawn and lying in their laps. So passed the night.

One or another dozed occasionally. There was no sound sleep. As dawn began to gray and fade in through the timber, a guttural voice, in some jargon Johnson could not comprehend, shouted at them from out in the oak brush.

"That's Kiowa," said Dewey. His usually placid voice had an edge that cut through its calm. The husky Chickasaw sounded as if his nerves were getting a little jangled.

Millar shouted something back in Cherokee, which neither Johnson nor any of the others could understand either. The Lighthorse captain threw back his head then and uttered a loud and challenging turkey gobble. There was another shout, in Kiowa, from the brush, and someone out there fired a shot. The bullet tore through the coals of their smoldering fire, showering sparks up into the gray daylight.

"Hey! That's enough of that!" Millar shouted, this time in English. "Somebody is going to get hurt!"

None of the Lighthorsemen raised a firearm.

From behind the tangle of greenbrier, barely twenty yards from camp, a feathered Plains warrior stood up. He was grinning. He said something in good-humored Kiowa and another warrior rose from the brush on the opposite side of the camp.

This one, past middle age and as ugly as Choctaw Buck Tom, wore shoulder-length hair and face paint. He spoke English.

"You come to talk?" he asked.

"We sure didn't come for no shooting match," Millar declared. "Bring your boys in. Let's make smoke."

The older warrior did not move. "Ou-poum-koudl," he said, gesturing toward himself.

Millar, then the other four Lighthorsemen, stood up.

"Pleased to meet you," the captain said. "I'm Millar Stone."

The Kiowa who had introduced himself nodded at his companion opposite. "He Koc'-kúoc."

The younger warrior, wearing a friendly yet wolfish grin, gestured and three other warriors, surrounding the camp, stood up.

Millar surveyed them. "I see you didn't have us outnumbered," he said.

Ou-poum-koudl, quietly confident, said, "It was a standoff that way. But," he reminded the Lighthorse captain, "you are in our terrain."

Like being the home team in a ball game, Johnson thought.

Ou-poum-koudl pointed with his chin to a heavyset warrior about his own age. "That is Tou-nkih. There is Soc-e-tein, and 'Eimhoc'H'." He indicated the pair of warriors flanking Koc'-kúoc.

Koc'-kúoc pointed to the last two men introduced, and said, "Ph'-bih."

"He says they are his brothers," Ou-poum-koudl translated. "You *tseirou-kíh?*" He said the word with Kiowa accents, but it sounded enough like "Cherokee" for Johnson to understand it.

Millar nodded and began his own chin-pointing. "That's Lee Dewey. He's Chickasaw. This is Mutt Kiley, Seminole. That's Johnson Lott, Creek. And this ugly old codger here is Buck Tom, Choctaw." He beckoned, "You boys come on in and set down. Let's palaver."

As they all gathered around the fire, Millar began pulling out sacks of Bull Durham tobacco. He tossed one to each Kiowa.

"No pipe?" Ou-poum-koudl asked.

Millar Stone actually blushed. Johnson could see the red blood suffuse his sun-browned face.

"I guess we've got out of the habit of carrying the pipe," Millar said. "You fellows got one?"

Ou-poum-koudl relayed the request in Kiowa. Koc'-kúoc reached into the pipe case slung alongside his arrow quiver and proudly brought out an ancient, hatchet-shaped cast-iron calumet. All the warriors, Kiowa and Five Tribes Lighthorsemen, sat down on the ground and Koc'-kúoc began filling the pipe-hatchet with tobacco from the Bull Durham sack he had been given. Johnson guessed that, since he was carrying the pipe and took the lead in preparing it, Koc'-kúoc was probably the elected leader of the five Kiowas.

Millar looked around the group speculatively, ending up with Ou-poum-koudl. "Could you give us some kind of handle for you fellows besides in Kiowa? I hate to be so impolite as not to call a man by his name, but my Cherokee tongue can't wrap itself around them Kiowa words."

The speaker of the Kiowas smiled sympathetically. "Yes," he consented. "My name means Adam's Apple." He had a prominent one. "Tou-nkih," he said, "means Fat Man." He was.

Adam's Apple nodded toward the pipe filler. "Koc'-kúoc means Badger." To his right was "Soc-e-tein—Blue Hail," and to Badger's left, " 'Eimhoc'H'—He Captures Them."

"Ph'-bih," said Badger.

"He reminds us that the three of them, Badger, Blue Hail, and He Captures Them, are brothers."

Badger was made like the stocky and lithe animal for which he was named. He was broad of body, with a homely but strongly friendly Kiowa face. Blue Hail was more handsome than his brother, perhaps more sober appearing, but Johnson thought the skin crinkles around his eyes, glinting with good-humored mischief, gave him away—he was the jokester. Johnson would have bet that it had been Blue Hail who had shot into the fire.

He Captures Them was taller than either of his brothers. He was strikingly handsome, slender and elegant, totally humorless and sober. Badger, with his bare fingers, picked a live coal from among the ashes and, ceremonially, fired up the pipe. He blew smoke to the four directions, to grandfather sun and mother earth, and passed the pipe to Millar who, somewhat awkwardly, repeated the maneuver.

Coughing a little from the heat and acrid strength of the smoke, Millar started the pipe around the circle. "I guess us Cherokees have got a little out of practice on the pipe ceremony," he apologized, "and I broke myself of the tobacco habit. But that sure don't mean that we're not eager to make smoke and talk with you folks. We come to invite you to a big Indian Fair we're going to have up in Muskogee in August."

The pipe had passed to Fat Man who, in spite of his folds of spare flesh, had great dignity, and seemed amicable and sociable. From him, Buck Tom received the pipe, smoked, and passed it on to Adam's Apple. As he smoked, Buck asked, "You the *alikchi*? The medicine man?"

Adam's Apple nodded. Buck grinned at Millar. "It takes one to know one," he said.

No one had replied to the invitation, so Millar expanded, "The Cherokees, Choctaws, Chickasaws, Seminoles, and Creeks will be there, along with a lot of our other friends; the Sac and Fox, Senecas, Quapaws, Yuchis, Delawares—them and you folks will be our guests. We'll furnish all the groceries and firewood. All you need to bring is yourselves and your tepees. We'd like for you to persuade the Comanches to come, if you can."

Adam's Apple put this into Kiowa and, after a silence, Badger spoke. Adam's Apple translated, "We would need to go back and discuss this with our people, with the old men."

Badger spoke again. Adam's Apple said, "He reminds me that his brother, He Captures Them, is married to a Comanche woman."

There was a long time of sitting during which the pipe smoking was finished. Badger emptied its ashes into his hand and carefully sprinkled them among the coals and ashes of the Lighthorsemen's fire. With hand signs, he murmured something which sounded reverent. Johnson knew the signs for "great" and "mystery." With the pointing upward he heard the word *Dawkeah,* which he guessed would be the Kiowa name for the Creek *Essaugeta Emissee,* the master of breath.

The young Lighthorseman remembered a trader named Nak-wíyv, a Creek who had traveled much among the Western Plains tribes, and had taught him some of these signs when he was a boy. Johnson resolved to hunt Nak-wíyv up during the Green Corn Dance at Hickory square ground and refresh his memory of these signs before the Indian Fair—if the Kiowas and Comanches could be persuaded to come.

The five Kiowas began speaking softly among themselves and Adam's Apple reported, "We are talking about a Cherokee man who visited the Kiowas a long time ago. I do not know his name, but it is told that he was the man who invented the Cherokees' 'talking leaves.' He was on his way to Mexico to seek some of his Cherokee brothers who had gone there to live, but he got sick and died. My father said that his body was left in the cave where he got sick, not far from here, on Skywalker Mountain."

Millar Stone sat up alertly. "That could have been Sequoyah. Nobody knows what really happened to him after he left his place down by Sallisaw." He asked Adam's Apple, "Could you take me to that place?"

There was more conversation in Kiowa before Adam's Apple answered, "We have agreed that it is not a good thing to disturb the bones of the dead, but we can tell you how to find that cave if you want to go there."

Buck Tom was showing Blue Hail how to take the cigarette papers from the packet attached to the Bull Durham sack and roll a cigarette. At once, all the Kiowas were at it, with sufficient success so that they were soon all lighting up and smoking the quirleys they had made. Good-humoredly, they passed across the bags Millar had given them. Each of the Lighthorsemen rolled a cigarette, lit it, and returned the borrowed Bull Durham sacks. Everyone puffed away and the still air became blue with smoke.

Buck Tom asked pleasantly, "How come you all shot at us? Then didn't come in for the kill? We were sitting ducks."

Adam's Apple explained, "We are a hunting party, not a war party. Some of us have made vows not to take any scalps until we have meat. Blue Hail shot into the fire just to see if you would run."

"You were checking on our nerves," Dewey drawled.

"We wanted to see if you would stay like men, or run like cowards," Adam's Apple said.

"Just curious," Mutt said wryly.

Adam's Apple nodded. "Badger had gone up on the mountain where he had gone five years ago to seek his medicine and his name. He saw you coming down through Stumbling Bear Pass, and watched you a long time. We wondered why five strange Indians in white men's clothes were coming into our country. We knew that you were not white men. We knew, when you got close, that you were from different tribes. It was confusing to us."

"I'm the Chickasaw here," Dewey said blandly. "Why are you mad at the Chickasaws?"

Adam's Apple looked puzzled. "We are not mad at the

Chickasaws. We are not really angry at anyone, except the *tejanos* and the white soldiers."

Badger cut into the talk in Kiowa and after more discussion in that strangely guttural, glottal tongue, Adam's Apple said, "Badger thinks we have all agreed that we should not talk anymore now. We will go to take what you have said before our people. After one sleep, we will meet you at the foot of Saddle Mountain. There it is yonder." He pointed with his chin at a pair of contiguous peaks abutted together like the pommel, seat, and cantle of a saddle. He hazarded, "Maybe we can bring some Comanches with us."

As the Kiowas brought the horses in from the brush, Adam's Apple said, "If you will keep on riding around the edge of this mountain, pretty soon you will come to a high plain that has a long lifting of red rocks curling through it. Those rocks look like a thick buffalo gut that has been pulled out bloody, with a little white fat on it. The end of those rocks points to Skywalker Mountain, and the cave containing the bones is almost at its top. Two big boulders lean together to make the cave's mouth. There are sure to be rattlesnakes there."

The Kiowas rode off, Badger leading, followed by his two brothers, then Fat Man and Adam's Apple. Before they were out of sight they had gathered together and were talking animatedly as they rode. The Lighthorsemen did not dally there among the blackjacks, but gathered their wits and their gear and struck out. They circled the skirt of the mountain that bordered Stumbling Bear Pass to arrive at a high plain covered with bright yellow flowers.

The uplift to their left was crowned with ramparts and battlements of ancient granite. They swam their horses across a stream some twenty feet wide and very deep. Its clear water was transparent, the bottom of its gorge covered with light tan sand. Fish, blue channel cats and perch, were abundant in the clear water, so they stopped, caught their dinner, and cooked it.

In the shade of leafy American elms they lay down and slept an hour to make up for last night's wakefulness. Then came a stretch of easy riding, through mountains kept clear of underbrush by the nibbling and grazing of deer, antelope and wild horses, and the burn-offs of occasional lightning-set prairie fires.

Rounding rugged battlements from the heights of which the earth had been washed away, they came upon the mountain pasture with its long gut of spilled-out granite, red as drying buffalo blood, yellowed and whitened by algae and lichens. Bleached tree branches littered the *rincones* between the shallow pasture ridges, swept there by summer rains that flooded this plain. Here, the dominant granite ridge twisted and curled its way through knee-high grass to peter out at the plain's edge, pointing directly toward the highest of three sugar-loaf peaks lapped against each other in the distance.

From where they sat resting in their saddles no detail of the mountains was clearly discernible in the afternoon haze, but they rode on toward what they knew must be Skywalker Mountain through a growth of cedars rising from the banks of another small creek. Selecting the rockiest plateau visible on the sloping mountain's side, they began the gradual climb ascending to it. They spread out to ride shouting distance apart. It was Dewey who, late in the afternoon's climbing, saw the cave's entrance.

A triangle framed by leaning boulders, as the Kiowas had described it, the entrance rose to a peak some five feet high above a dirt-covered granite shelf that thrust out like a porch in front of the cave. Beyond, the interior faded to disappear in a maw of stygian black. Leaving their horses, they fired dry cedar branches brought from the grove below and entered the cave.

Inside, as their eyes accustomed to the reduced light, they found what they sought. A skeleton lay propped against the rocky west wall. Some of its bones had been disjointed by prowling animals, but it remained mostly intact, and it was apparent why. The cave was populous with rattlesnakes.

Torpid diamond-backed rattlers lay about the cave den, resting in the cool dark. The Lighthorsemen moved toward the skeleton through its guardian legion of drowsy serpents. The reptilian odor of the low cave was a strong stench.

"Don't stir them up too much," Millar cautioned. "The old-time Cherokees considered them sacred messengers from the underworld."

A silver medallion hung from a chain wound around the skeleton's neck bones, reflecting the cedar torchlight. Millar leaned to examine it.

"It is a gift that was given to Sequoyah by the Cherokee tribe," Millar said, "for developing our written language. His syllabary made us able to print the Cherokee *Phoenix* in Georgia, and the *Advocate* newspaper in Tahlequah. His 'talking leaves' made our Cherokees a literate people." The Lighthorse captain backed away a step and stood silent in respect. "Look at that leg bone, boys," he said.

The bone, slightly angled, had long ago been broken and had healed crookedly. "Sequoyah was lame," Millar said. "He limped on one bent leg, broke when he was a youngster. It never did heal straight."

They stood together, looking down at the bones. One of the snakes, short and thick, near Johnson's right boot, coiled lazily and began its warning rattle. Johnson moved cautiously away from it.

"Not a good place to spend the night." Buck Tom laughed nervously.

"It would be a real honor to say we'd spent the night with Sequoyah," Millar said half seriously.

"May-y-be," Dewey responded coolly, "but I don't think I could tolerate the company he's keeping now." He eased back toward the cave's entrance.

"No, I expect not," Millar noted. The spooky torchlight flickering on the cavern walls kept on alerting the dormant rattlesnakes. Heat from the five blazing cedar faggots was beginning to warm the serpent-stinking air of the cave, further enlivening its reptile occupants. The Lighthorsemen carefully backed out of the cave onto its granite-floored patio.

Here in the late afternoon sunlight, Johnson immediately found himself breathing easier. Mutt was ready to go. He removed his Union forager's cap and wiped away a thin sheen of sweat glistening on his forehead.

"Rattlesnakes and owls give me the willywaws," he admitted. "Maybe there's nothing to the old *por'ru* beliefs that the spirits of the departed turn into owls and consort with serpents, but I'd just as soon not stick around here to find out for sure."

Millar suggested, "Let's camp for tonight alongside that last creek we crossed. It's running sweet water, and my stomach is speaking up in favor of another fried fish supper."

That camp, pitched on the bank of Cache Creek, gave them a full rest from the past night's wakefulness and worry. With the rising sun, they broke camp, riding on toward Saddle Mountain. Emerging from the cedars into scrub-oak timber in the early morning light, Johnson caught sight of a shadow at the timber's edge. It was tall and slender, moving gently across the grass, and for an instant Johnson could not believe what he was seeing.

It was the shadow of Martha Lewis.

Spurring Pos'ketv, he rode toward it with a clatter of hoofs. It disappeared. What he had seen was only a shape of leaves that grew from a sapling, throwing a long early-morning shadow on the ground and, on closer inspection, it bore no resemblance whatever to Martha Lewis. Johnson rode, shamefaced, back to the Lighthorsemen.

"What got into you?" queried Millar. "You feel an urgent call of nature?"

Johnson alibied sheepishly, "I guess ol' Pos'ketv is full of ginger. He kind of got away from me there for a minute."

But as the morning latened, he found that whatever had

plagued him had not been an isolated instance, for he frequently saw her before him: an outline of her figure in the tumbled rivers of boulders, fallen together and fixed in place by time on the sun-swept mountainsides, the fine-featured contours of her face, as clearly visible as a daguerreotype image in the fluffy-edged cottony white clouds against a deep blue sky.

What is ailing me? he thought. But he knew well enough, for he felt sick in spirit from the long lonesomes plaguing at him. His longings became anguish. He could see her face or her shape everywhere. Everything he looked at seemed in some way to remind him of Martha, until their noon crossing of a narrow, frothing race of white water cascading down from the steep side of Saddle Mountain. There the charge of the Kiowa and Comanche warriors swept everything else from his mind.

They came pouring out from concealment behind giant granite boulders where the mountain reared up out of the earth—war-painted, war-bonneted, an iridescent column of feathers, buckskin, and beads. Mounted on painted war ponies, the column of bedizened Plains nomads thundered down the mountainside, overwhelming the bewildered clot of caught-short Lighthorsemen.

Wool-gathering has cost me my life, Johnson thought numbly. All five of the emissaries of the Civilized Tribes were held transfixed by the charging Indians, who drove within yards of the noisy watercourse, then twisted away to become a kaleidoscope of whirling bright colors, riding like devils. Then an Indian caught a noose woven into the mane of his spotted pony and completely disappeared on its far side. He came crawling under its belly while the pony ran at top speed, then climbed up the near side to again ride astride.

Every rider performed acrobatics on his flashing mount. Using only the hair rings woven into manes and the horses' braided tails, they bounced and bounded, somersaulted, swept down to pick up warriors who fell from their horses to lie flat on the ground simulating wounds, rode laid out on their backs with their heads hanging over the horses' rumps, stood up, sat down, and rode backward, fiends howling in a cacophonic din of war cries, tremolos, wild singing, and shouting.

The column of Kiowas and Comanches spiraled into its own center, turned upon itself and began circling outward while its Cherokee, Choctaw, Chickasaw, Creek, and Seminole observers sat watching and trying to regain their composure. After the utter quiet of the long morning ride, the sudden violence of the warriors' shrieks and shouts and their barbaric display was wholly unnerving.

Millar Stone sat his horse phlegmatically until the spiral unwound itself outward, then spurred his horse with a yell and a turkey gobble to fall in at the end of the line of hard-charging warriors. The four other Lighthorsemen followed. Their Chickasaw horses were the equal of the Comanche and Kiowa war ponies, matching their hell-bent racing pace, and the column spiraled inward again with the Lighthorsemen's yells contributing to the pandemonium, although the five omitted the fancy riding tricks the wild Indians were demonstrating.

Exiting the swirling spiral, the leader of the foofaraw gave some unseen signal and the hell-bent but tightly disciplined column of warriors turned into a boiling mill. The yelling and howling around the Lighthorsemen tapered to become shouted laughter, and Badger rode among them, his laughter and explosive bursts of Kiowa made comprehensible by his beckoning as he led them off, still at full gallop, around the near shoulder of Saddle Mountain.

There the women had gathered. Pots were boiling and, on spits over smoking charcoal, a brace of antelope roasted. The women passed out wooden bowls and buffalo-horn spoons and the feasting began. Gnawing off a chunk of antelope meat, savory with juices, Millar admitted, "You sure upwinded us."

Here the smell of cooking smoke was redolent. The prevailing southerly breeze swept it up into the canyons of the mountains to the north with such a draft that no odor from the

barbecue and boiling frybread could have reached the
Lighthorsemen. Nevertheless, Johnson could see that all this
activity was going on within a mile of the narrow Saddle
Mountain cascade crossing where the wild Indians had surprised them. It was embarrassing to him, and clearly pleasing
to the Plains people, that they had taken the "civilized" Indians unawares.

It was gratifying to hear Adam's Apple admit while they ate
that, "You put us at a disadvantage over there by the Stumbling Bear Pass. We thought you would run, and we might
have chased you and killed you. But you surprised us with
your courage and turned that encounter into a council. We decided we had to redeem our honor by surprising you here."

Millar patted his full stomach. "You couldn't have picked a
pleasanter way to do it."

While chattering women cleared away the leftovers of the
feast, meat and bread and blueberry dumplings, carrying
stacks of bowls, cooking pots, and horn spoons off to the white-
water race for washing, the warriors assembled themselves to
listen to what the Lighthorsemen had to say. Millar selected
Dewey to start, presenting him as, "Our Chickasaw Lighthorse policeman from down around Colbert's Ferry. You Comanches and Kiowas know that Chickasaw Red River country
like you know your own horse's backs, and you keep it so well
curried us Five Tribes Indians have got to calling it 'Scalp
Alley.' What do you do with all the hair you raise down
there?"

Laughter was his only answer. Dewey challenged them,
"Bring your fastest horses to the Indian Fair at Muskogee. We
will run races, and I believe that we can beat you. We are better at winning horse races than you are at lifting scalps."

There were gutturaled "houghs" which Johnson took as an
expression of agreement to bring horses to Muskogee—but not
agreement that they would be beaten. There were obviously
many English-speakers among the Plains warriors. Translation
of Dewey's and Millar's statements had been instant and John-

son saw flashing hand signs which he was too rusty to comprehend. By the time he recalled the meaning of a single sign a
dozen others had been made, losing him in confusion.

Mutt Kiley followed Dewey, reminding them that, "We will
have a crafts building where you can show your beadwork,
buckskin shirts and dresses, quillwork and ornaments made of
silver, copper, and brass. You can sell those objects if you
wish to."

Johnson did not know what to say. He got up diffidently
when Millar motioned him out in front of the crowd. He stood
uncertainly, shifting his weight from one foot to the other,
then finally, naïve and unpretentious, began, "There is a carnival at the fair every year, with great wheels, some of them laying flat, some standing up edgewise. They carry things like
bright-painted wagon boxes, and horses made of wood. All
kinds of dizzy ways to ride that you and your children will
hardly believe. I remember what amazing things they were to
me the first time I ever saw them."

He saw that he had caused quite a stir. No one had any idea
what he was talking about. The question sign, a shaken right
hand above the right shoulder, was flashing everywhere, but
Johnson did not know how to explain the carnival any better,
so, in a noisy hubbub of talk, he sat down.

Buck Tom, a grin stretched across his ugly face, widening
the thick-lipped mouth beneath his spatulate nose, got up to
take his turn. "We have a show every afternoon in front of the
board seats they call a grandstand. You can show off your riding tricks there, and do fancy dances. Your warriors can wear
their sunburst bustles. Your pretty women can show off their
buckskin dresses, making their long fringes shake in that be-
witching way when they dance."

Millar got up to conclude. "The main thing, that's serious
and urgent, is that the most important men of both our peoples
will have plenty of time to sit in council. Maybe while they
make smoke and talk they can work out some of the problems
that separate us. These fractious incidents that happen along

our borders, especially over in the Chickasaw country, cause fighting in which folks get hurt and killed."

The two oldest chieftains present, Charging Bear of the Kiowas and Buffalo Coat of the Comanches, spoke for the Plains people.

"You eastern Indians," said Charging Bear, "are different from us. You have strange ways. We wear the warbonnet. You do not. I have seen your men wearing cloth wrapped around their heads—a turban, we have heard that you call it. We see the white women wearing things like that. We live in lodges made of the skin of the buffalo. You live in little houses like those of the whites, only not so big and fine."

"That's true," Millar replied. "We do a lot of things pretty much the way the whites do. Back in the 1830s our houses in the South were big and fine, often finer than the white men's houses. That's why they took our houses and drove us out here."

Charging Bear continued to protest. "When we dance we dress up in colored blankets, beaded buckskin, bright feathers, all our finery, and we wear dance bells. When our young men kick up the dust they make music with those bells on their legs and arms. When you dance you wear the same clothes you wear every day—usually old clothes the white men have thrown away. And you only trot around the fire, with dull songs. No bells jingling, just a few rocks making a clonking rattle in turtle shells some of your women tie to their legs."

The Comanche elder, Buffalo Coat, his blanket slung with casual grace across his shoulder and falling in neat folds over his bandy legs, asserted, "You have seen us ride. When we ride we do many things that are exciting to watch and good to use in a fight. When you ride you cannot do any of those things. You just ride—like the white men do."

"I've seen these differences," Millar acknowledged, "but they are trifling, piddling things—things on the outside," he insisted stubbornly. "Inside, underneath all that, I think we are more alike than we are different. That's what needs to be talked about when we get together in Muskogee. After all, we are all Indians, and we ought to be able to get along together."

Charging Bear and Buffalo Coat sat thinking about this, and fell into a discussion between themselves. In flowing Kiowa, in Comanche splintery with consonants, their graceful hands converting every thought into Plains signs, they talked and invited the opinion of others around the circle until at last Charging Bear delivered their verdict. They had agreed that they themselves, Comanche and Kiowa, had once been bitter enemies. "But we decided that we would stop fighting," said Charging Bear. "Now we are strong friends. Maybe it will be possible for us to be friends with you Indians who the white-eyes call 'civilized.' We will come to your fair in Muskogee during the heat moon."

Charging Bear's downbrushing right hand crossed the palm of his left, signifying "this finished it," and Buffalo Coat made the *yes* downstroke with fist and pointing finger. He grunted a confirming, "Hough!"

The council was over.

CHAPTER 7

As the Lighthorsemen prepared to leave, Blue Hail, Badger, He Captures Them, Fat Man, and Adam's Apple gathered with them. With hand-shaking all around, sign talk, and much chatter, Adam's Apple delivered the consensus of their advice.

He said, pointing north, "That is not the best way to start out from Saddle Mountain."

The closed fingers of his hand rose obliquely upward, emphasizing the great distance to be traveled. "No one should travel between our country and those Creek lands by that California Trail. It is too far."

Turning toward the northeast with a wide sweep of his right arm, Adam's Apple said, "There is an old trail the Spaniards from Mexico used to use. It goes to the place where the big muddy river, the Canadian, begins to flow east. From there the river will take you to the *tejano* road that has the white man's iron road built beside it."

The Lighthorsemen then made their departure, with Millar insisting, "Be sure you got that Kiowa's directions straight, Johnson. You're the one going back to Muskogee. You'll have to report to Nathan."

Mutt was restraining an impatient horse that seemed to anticipate home pastures. "I'm going to hightail it for Barking Water, my place at Wewoka," Mutt declared. "If all three of my boys caught the flu, then maybe my wife caught it . . ."

"Quit worrying!" Millar urged. "One of that passel of kids and grandkids around my place is always runny-nosed, and my wife is worrying about the one ailing and all the others at the same time. I'll tell you, Mutt, why don't you bring your wife and the kids up to the fair. You too, Dewey. I'll even bring that troupe of medicine show Indians I've sired. Now, ol' Buck here—"

"My kids are all long grown up and gone," Buck Tom said with a laugh, "and I'm glad of it. I'll bring my old lady. We'll have us a time."

"That's real fine," Millar declared, and they parted, scattering for home.

The M. K. & T., the Missouri, Kansas, and Texas, was known as the Katy Railroad. *Talahina,* the Choctaws called it —their word for iron road. In two long days in the saddle Johnson rode almost as straight as the crow flies to Adam's Apple's "big muddy river," then followed the *talahina* on north to Muskogee. He went directly to see Nathan Able.

Having related the details of the Saddle Mountain council, he pressed another question.

"Mr. Able, can I take time off to go to the Green Corn Dance?" He stood uncomfortably, shifting his weight self-consciously, and began a circuitous justification. "It starts the Creek new year, you know, and there isn't anything more important to us who like the old Indian ways . . ."

The agent leaned back, locking his fingers across his lean belly as he asked, "Which square ground would you intend to visit, Private Lott?"

"Hickory, down by old North Fork Town."

"That will likely be where Buster Vixico and his partisans will congregate. Will it not?"

"Yes, sir. We both grew up down there. Buster and I played ball together for Hickory square ground."

"Then instead of taking time off and losing your pay, such as it is, Johnson," Able said, "why not consider it a part of your duties. As I suggested before you all went south to the Wichitas, we need to try to patrol such a gathering. I'll assign you to police the Hickory square ground during the Green

Corn Festival. You are Creek, fluent in the Muscogee tongue—
the very man most qualified for such an assignment."

Johnson relaxed. He grinned diffidently. "Thank you, Mr.
Able."

The agent turned to his desk and his paper work. "Play a
good ball game," he proposed. "Perhaps if you assist Vixico
on a few plays, he'll feel less bitterly toward you for having
confiscated his whiskey a while back."

Johnson doubted that, but he walked on back to the stable
to saddle his Chickasaw stallion Pos'ketv. He paused beside
the handsome chestnut mare and promptly gave her the name
Hoktecákv. With reason, he thought, for the Chickasaw
mare's first rider since he had acquired her was surely, he
deeply hoped, going to be a fine lady. He put a leading halter
on the mare.

As he rode back toward the big Agency house, leading Hoktecákv, Johnson pulled up thoughtfully. He dismounted, gave
Pos'ketv's reins a turn around the back porch post, and went
into the kitchen. Auntie Kerfetu was there, bent over at a sharp
angle, looking at a cake baking in the oven.

Johnson cleared his throat guiltily. She stood up, facing him
with an abruptness that made him sure she had known he was
there all the time.

"Auntie Kerfetu," he began uncertainly.

"You are fidgety, Johnson Lott," she accused. "Perhaps you
are feeling guilty about something."

"Ah." He determinedly shook his head. "I was wondering if
you are going down to the Hickory square ground—"

"For the Green Corn ceremony." She nodded brusquely and
stared at him. The angular housekeeper was almost as tall as
he was. "You know I have never missed one since before you
were born. So why are you asking?"

He felt a flush of heat mottle his face. "I thought," Johnson
said diffidently, "we might talk—"

"About blue jays?" She still stared, curious and accusing.

"Ah." He winced as from a blow. "No—ah—it is too stuffy

and hot in here." He gave up, protesting, and turned and left the kitchen. Mounting with the smooth grace of a man more comfortable in the saddle than afoot, he urged Pos'ketv down the yard road, bringing Hoktecákv willingly along behind.

He recovered his aplomb while riding down the Texas Road, but when he reached the Lewises' cabin the bashfulness swept in on him again. Johnson Lott had, in all his life, never asked a girl for a favor. He reminded himself that Martha had been the one first to express her interest and to say that she would like to go. He reminded himself that, in a sense, he had already confirmed their going, just before he had run out of her yard on the way to the Wichitas.

But he had not given her time to reply. Now he was confronted with the time of truth. Would she really want to go, or had her expressed interest and desire to go been only a pretense? Perhaps to flatter him, to make him feel good? He could truthfully conceive of no reason why any girl would want to go anywhere with him. Especially, why would this slender girl, of whom he had dreamed, with her fine features, her pale pink hands and long, sensitive fingers, want to go with him to camp out at a stomp dance?

She came out of the house as soon as she heard the clomping hoofs of his two horses coming into the yard. She stood staring up at him, her face flushed a welcoming pink even more attractive than the pinkness of her beautiful, long-fingered hands.

She looked at Hoktecákv and said, "What a beautiful horse."

"I brought her for you," he said. Flustered, his heart beating fast and hard, he could not bring himself to ask in a way that would fetch a definite yes or no answer.

Instead, he hedged. "The Green Corn Dance starts day after tomorrow."

"Well"—she looked away, her lips prim and firm—"I don't know. I'd like to go." She was surely blushing as she looked back up at him, directly into his eyes. "We'll have to ask Daddy."

Johnson saw her father then, rushing up from the cowshed. He had a momentary fear that Silan Lewis was coming toward them belligerently, which was instantly dispelled by Lewis's warm greeting.

"Get down, get down," the homesteader invited. "I was just going out to do the evening milking."

While Johnson dismounted, unsaddled, and put up his horses, Lewis waited, then hurried back to his chores. Johnson followed, walking on out to the homesteader's new peeled-pole and wattle cowshed, where the musical twang of fresh milk striking the bottom of the empty metal bucket was fast assuming deeper tones as the long, accurate streams of Silan Lewis's milking filled the pail with warm, fragrant, creamy milk.

To avoid standing around and disturbing the already-nervous Jersey beside which the homesteader knelt, Johnson lifted another empty pail from its hanging nail and went off to the hen house to gather eggs. He carried them in to Martha, arriving at the same time Silan arrived with the milk.

Supper was fresh milk with fried mush and molasses.

"I hate to shoot game at this time of the summer," Lewis acknowledged, filling the supper table silence. "So often the squirrels and rabbits are full of young, and it is too hot to preserve anything as large as a deer. The meat spoils before we can eat it all. This next winter we'll butcher a hog and cure the hams, bacon, and sidemeat. That should see us through to next summer."

Johnson helped Martha clear away the dishes, and she got out the books. The evening passed in study, and everyone went to bed, Johnson in his accustomed place among the oaks beside the horse pen. The matter of the Green Corn Dance was never raised.

The next morning Johnson went with the settler to his ripened cornfield, helping him harvest the silky tasseled ears of new corn.

"The crop matured amazingly well," Martha's father exulted, "in spite of being planted a little late. It has been a perfect corn year," he declared elatedly, "hot and humid. I could almost hear it growing, particularly at night, crackling and popping as the stalks shot up in the field!"

Silan Lewis's good humor over the success of his corn crop gave Johnson the courage to try. "Every year my people have a ceremony of thanks," he said, "when we finish up last year's corn and harvest the new."

"An admirable custom," said Lewis. "Man should surely give thanks for his blessings."

Johnson felt encouraged. He seemed to be doing better than he had feared that he would. "I came by—" He hesitated. "I expect you heard Martha say that first evening we were studying that she would like to go to it. Anyway, I sure would like to take her."

Lewis's reluctance surfaced at once. "Now, I don't know about that. I recall hearing her mention it. You surely wouldn't plan to be gone overnight?"

"Yes, we would." Johnson felt supplicant and stubborn at the same time. "The Creek ladies would chaperone Martha. I'll have to be off some with the *tustannuggee,* the warriors." As the word left him he suddenly felt abashed, dismayed, disconcerted, perhaps as a result of what the old Kiowa Charging Bear had said down in the Wichitas. No one, seeing him in these worn-out white-man clothes, could think of him as a Creek warrior!

But perhaps Silan Lewis saw him differently—as a proud, tall, muscular, brown-skinned young man, wearing a broad black hat with a long and belligerent turkey feather thrust rakishly in its brim—for Johnson embarrassingly felt that he could see something like admiration in Lewis's eyes as he reluctantly consented. "If you're sure that she'll be all right, and if Martha is sure that she wants to go—"

He feels sorry for me, Johnson thought unreasonably, but he was too glad at having even this reluctant permission to let anything alter success. When they returned to the cabin with armloads of roasting ears, Martha firmly expressed her desire to go. After another night of study, Martha enthusiastically dug through the household goods, now stored under the brush arbor, to find the sidesaddle she had mentioned at their first meeting. Finding it, she uncovered it lovingly, for it had been her mother's. Johnson dusted it carefully, cinched it firmly on Hoktecákv, and they set off for North Fork Town in a cloud of ecstasy.

Johnson knew he would never forget that ride. Everything seemed hazed in a special glowing kind of glory. Martha Ann chattered cheerfully all the way. Birds sang for them. A gentle wind rustled the full green, thick leaves of the summer trees. The clear streams they forded gurgled and laughed over round brown stones as though responding to the joy he felt. Approaching Hickory square ground, they let the Chickasaw horses run free across the waving foxtail grass of the Canadian flood plain, then crossed the wide river with its shallow currents and broad, red expanse of sandbars.

She rode like a princess, balanced easily, gracefully in the sidesaddle, her long calico skirt draped modestly to cover her slender legs, her waist bending and pliant to the elegant Chickasaw mare's every rhythmic step. As they rode out of the river, onto the square ground, Johnson led her promptly to the willow-covered arbor where he expected to find Auntie Kerfetu. Beneath the arbor, partitioned with blankets and quilts to provide sleeping quarters, the Agency housekeeper should be camping with her brother, his wife, and their four youngsters.

She was there. Thankfully, Johnson stepped down to approach the curious Creek woman who stood at the edge of the arbor, alertly observing their arrival. Auntie Kerfetu kept her hands still, hidden deep in the folds of her apron, but her eyes were active, examining every detail of the girl perched high in the sidesaddle on the horse now halted beside the withers of policeman Johnson Lott's mount.

"Good evening," Johnson greeted Auntie Kerfetu politely.

She responded with a silent nod. Her spritely eyes contained something, certainly new, a feeling that Johnson could not read.

"My brother *tustannuggee* is not here?" Johnson asked.

Auntie Kerfetu said, "Cu'sē, my brother, who is indeed a warrior, has taken the wagon down along the river to get a load of firewood."

"His wife and his children—"

"Have gone along to help him."

Johnson turned. "This is Martha Ann Lewis," he explained. "She is not familiar with our ways—"

"A blessing if she is not familiar with your ways." The look in Auntie Kerfetu's eyes was now fathomable, comprehending and wise, but friendly. "A rough Lighthorse policeman is bad company for a young lady. Get down, Martha Ann. Come here and stand behind me in the brush arbor and I will protect you from him."

Martha Ann's laughter sounded to Johnson Lott like the faraway ringing of jubilant bells. She slid to the ground from the sidesaddle and, as she walked toward Auntie Kerfetu, the smiling Creek woman extracted her hands from her apron and took hold of Martha's hands. Johnson felt a flush of relief that warmed his face.

He ducked his head and awkwardly toed the ground with a black boot, knowing that he must look like a backward small boy. "I was wondering," he asked, "if she—Martha Ann—Miss Lewis—could stay with you?"

"We have plenty room for, as you put it, all three of her," Auntie Kerfetu teased him amiably.

"I will go find the wagon and help load the firewood," he said.

"Do not expect to sleep here," Auntie warned him. "We have no room for hunters of blue jays, who only conceal the criminals they find."

Sheepishly, and glad to escape, Johnson rode away hearing

Martha ask, "What can I do to help?" and Auntie Kerfetu's voice saying, "I am baking sweet potatoes . . ."

As pleased as he was at Martha's ready acceptance, Johnson found another concern deepening. Auntie Kerfetu's jibes about the Younger's Bend whiskey maker were inevitably going to fall on the ears of somebody who knew what she meant, or would go to the trouble to find out. Now, too, that he had undertaken to reveal Martha Ann Lewis to the agent's Creek housekeeper, he suspected that curious Auntie Kerfetu would not take long in finding out all about Martha and her father. Johnson began to have the dreadful feeling that this whole rope of sand was about to disintegrate in his hands.

He found the wagon easily and helped Auntie's brother Cu'sē, his wife, and their youngsters load it full of whitened driftwood from the banks and sandy bars of the river. They returned to camp and Johnson busied himself with axe and bucksaw, cutting and splitting the firewood. The meal that followed, which Johnson was invited to join, was pleasant enough, though he ate only a little *humpeta hutke*—white food, or hominy—in preparation for the purification rite awaiting him. It was a little unpleasant, too, for Cu'sē's wife, Híwv, had recently joined the white man's church and taken the Christian name Rebecca. Now she spent time in arguing with her husband that they should not expose their children to the heathen ceremonies of the square ground until they were old enough to decide for themselves which way they wanted to follow.

Híwv, Rebecca, was appealing to Martha Ann to side with her, and Johnson had the feeling that Martha might have done so had she felt less strange and new in these surroundings. He felt a little like an outcast himself as he left Cu'sē's camp to seek the medicine man and purify himself for the *heniha* dance. In the secrecy of the *chokofa* he partook the black drink, rested for a while, then smoked with others who were preparing themselves.

With the rising of the moon, he made his way to the square ground for the *heniha*. Passing Cu'sē's arbor, he saw Martha and Auntie Kerfetu sitting facing each other across the long supper table in the front of the arbor. They were talking. He walked slowly, then, guiltily, stopped completely in the shadows. From this concealment, he could hear Auntie Kerfetu gossiping, "I helped his mother *hopúe ahecícetv,* to take care of him, when he was born. He was as bashful about coming as he has since been about staying!"

They were talking about him! Johnson was mortified. He slipped away, but the temptation to eavesdrop was too great. He slipped back quietly.

Auntie Kerfetu was saying, "I have no patience with my sister-in-law. Creeks who went to the white man's church used to be punished by whipping."

"But if it is a heathen religion—" Martha essayed hesitantly.

"It is not," Auntie contradicted hotly. "It concerns the sacred eternal fire, which our parents brought, burning, over the Trail of Tears, from the ancient Creek fires of our forefathers in Alabama."

"But you said 'sacred.' God is not a fire."

Through the oak leaves Johnson saw Auntie Kerfetu arise, take Martha's arm, and lead her to the edge of the square ground.

"There you see the fire," Auntie said, "in the middle of all the surrounding camps. Around it on all sides is a ridge of earth, made from years of gleanings, from all the times this ground has been swept and cleaned. The arbor on the west side is the chief's arbor. The one on the north is for the peace people. The south one is for the *tustannuggees,* the warriors. The one on this side is for everyone. The camps, like ours, are gathering places for families, for friends and relatives from distant places. It is more like a family reunion than something heathen."

"But you said they used to whip those who even went to the white man's church."

"That was a long time ago. Now we Creeks are getting a little more used to the ways of the whites, but I think our old

ways were the best. We used to start the festival at the time of
the July full moon, and it lasted eight days. Now, because so
many Creeks work at regular white people's jobs, we start on
Friday nearest the full moon, and it only lasts the next two
days. The most important time is when we kindle the new fire.
It is a time for forgetting bad things, forgiving old wrongs, for
new beginnings, for offering thanks to the master of breath for
the first fruits of our cornfields. Does that sound like something
heathen?"

"No," Martha admitted, "but—"

Out beside the chief's arbor old man Heléswv had risen
from his place. He began speaking in the Muscogee language.
Auntie Kerfetu said, "He is our chief medicine doctor, and he
says that he is glad to see that so many have been spared from
death and have gathered in this place. He says that we will
have many visitors, and they are welcome. He urges our young
people to avoid boisterousness and careless laughing for fear
our visitors might think they are being laughed at and be embarrassed.

"When friends come to our camp he wants us to share
whatever scanty fare we have with them. He tells us that when
our ancestors practiced these customs in their entirety they did
so with joy and glory, and although we have almost forgotten
these beloved ways he will attempt to carry them on as best he
can, and so continue to the end.

"You see now," Auntie said, "they have started dancing.
That is an Old Dance song they are singing, and the rhythm is
kept by the terrapin shells bound to some of the dancers' legs.
You see they always dance with their hearts nearest the fire,
and in a spiral symbolic of the earth joined to the sun."

"The earth—joined to the sun?" To Johnson, Martha
sounded only confused. "How—" she started to inquire.

"I cannot say any more," Auntie told her. "I have probably
talked too much already. Women are not supposed to talk
about sacred things. Come, we should go and sit where we can
see everything."

They moved out to the spectators' arbor to sit down, and Johnson followed until he could slip into place in the dance procession. Later, after midnight, he slipped away, quietly skirting the perimeter of the square ground, to find a place to lie down and rest in solitude.

With the feeling that he was becoming more and more separated from everyone, Johnson thought about the Crazy Snake warriors who, during the dancing, had avoided him completely. Earlier, he had sensed in Auntie Kerfetu, and in Cu'sē's family, a feeling that he had set himself apart from them. It started, he thought, back when I became a Lighthorse policeman. The presence here of Martha, who had come with him, seemed almost to have more to do with it. At least, Buster and the Crazy Snakes aren't drinking whiskey here, he contemplated. The religious influence of the Green Corn Dance—their respect for old man Heléswv's *ome-ispokógi* authority—was holding them in check. Johnson watched the changing patterns of the summer stars and the waning moon until he went to sleep.

He awakened in the morning and lay sensing the tempered pace of Busk activity. He could hear the measured strokes of the pole boys, sweeping and cleaning the square ground. The family camps were smothered in quiet. There would be no breakfast this morning. Both Pos'ketv and Hoktecákv grazed, browsing in the clearing near where Johnson lay, reminding him that Martha was sleeping, or newly awake, in the camp with Auntie Kerfetu and Cu'sē's family less than a hundred yards from where he lay. He could hear Heléswv's voice praying from the chief's arbor. An occasional small boy straggled past through the camp arbors, heading toward Heléswv's voice and instruction to be given there.

Johnson got up, dug through the saddlebag he had used as a pillow, in search of a clean cloth, and went off toward the river to wash himself and prepare for the day. As he began his ablutions, a buggy came out of the timber trail on the far side of the Canadian, rolled down to the river's edge, and launched out into the sluggish, roily current. The buggy came nearer, and Johnson recognized the slight man with moustache and goatee who drove it. Sure enough, it was Chief Tsch-kote himself.

Johnson finished washing, dried himself with the clean cloth, dressed, and moved to intersect the buggy's route. As it came tracking up out of the water, cutting deep ruts in the sandbars it crossed, Tsch-kote called out, whoaing his horse and pulling the buggy to a stop.

"Get in," he invited. "Ride into camp with me."

Johnson put a hand on the dashboard, booted the buggy's round iron step and swung upward. The buggy rocked downward precariously beneath his solid weight, righting itself as he sat down beside Tsch-kote. Johnson said nothing, and Tsch-kote commented, "I've not seen you since you left my office with the Choctaw to go fence cutting. Agent Able tells me you are doing a good job."

"We keep busy," Johnson admitted. His brain was busy. It was an opportunity, this coincidental happenstance. It seemed to Johnson a golden opportunity to resolve one, and maybe both, of his major problems at once. Surely Tsch-kote could not meet Martha Ann Lewis without becoming at once won over and sympathetic to her!

Chief Tsch-kote said, "Mr. Able and I have discussed the efficiency with which you intertribal policemen calmed down the Crazy Snake insurgency. That was impressive."

Johnson shook his head. "That is one of the things I need to talk over with you, Chief Tsch-kote. The Crazy Snakes are a long ways from being calm."

"Are they here, for this Green Corn ceremony?"

"Yes, sir."

"Are they making trouble?"

"No, sir."

"Good. The information I have indicates that their encampment over by Eufaula broke up peacefully after you Lighthorsemen departed. They went to their homes quietly without trading for any more whiskey. Have you seen any whiskey here?"

"No, sir. I expect they don't want to offend the *ispokógis,* but that whiskey is another thing we need to talk about."

Tsch-kote's slow old horse pulled in among the ceremonial square ground's camp arbors. "I'll take time to greet the people," Tsch-kote said, "then we can meet to discuss the things you mention. Do you have any idea where they get their whiskey?"

The buggy was now alongside Cu'sē's big brush arbor. Johnson swung down out of the slow-moving vehicle. "If you can wait just a minute here, sir," he urged, "there is someone I would like for you to meet."

Fetching Martha Ann was no problem. She was already coming out of the quilt-hung cubicle that had served as her bedroom. "I thought I heard your voice!" she exclaimed cheerfully. "Good morning!"

"Good morning," Johnson responded. Immediately, he was filled with the same brimming joy and swept with the same bashful reticence that seemed to possess him whenever he was in her presence. But he must not let himself be plagued with a tied tongue now. Another chance like this might be a long time in coming.

"Ah, Chief—Mr. Tsch-kote, this is Martha Ann Lewis. The chief here," he explained to Martha, "hired me to be a Lighthorseman."

"How do you do?" She offered her slender hand and Tsch-kote touched it politely.

"I could do with a few less problems,"—he smiled gently—"as Private Lott has probably told you."

"No," she said. "He hasn't—"

Johnson suspected she was going to say "told me anything about you," so he interrupted, "Miss Lewis is visiting here with Auntie Kerfetu."

"Certainly so refined a young woman could never be a

problem, as Auntie Kerfetu is not," Tsch-kote said. "I'm delighted to meet you."

Johnson began to sweat slightly, though the morning was not yet overwarm.

"We often have a few white visitors for our stomp dances," Tsch-kote commented, "but rarely one so comely. Your name 'Martha' is an Aramaic word with the connotation 'genteel.'"

"Thank you," Martha responded with the matter-of-fact bluntness with which Johnson had grown so familiar. "Everything so far is a confusing mystery to me. I've been told that women are not supposed to discuss religious things."

Tsch-kote's smile turned quizzical. With pursed lips, he said, "The old tribal taboos have a strong hold on many of our people."

They sat at the long table in the open half of Cu'sē's arbor. Tsch-kote said conversationally, "It is certain to be another hot day." He was clearly taken with Martha and enjoyed her frankness.

"Yes," Martha said. "My father has remarked often in recent weeks that it has been a splendid corn-growing summer."

Johnson began to sweat in earnest. Apprehension that Tsch-kote would ask where her father's corn crop was came surging up through him.

Instead, Tsch-kote sat quietly for a minute, as though collecting his thoughts. "There are several Busks held in the Creek Nation," he said. "Kashita, Tukabahchee—no two quite alike, or held exactly at the same time. I must go from here to Coweta. Their *archimagus* has sent out the broken days."

Martha looked quizzical.

"Broken sticks," Tsch-kote explained. "One for each day remaining until the festival. The head medicine maker sends them as soon as he is sure when it will be. The square ground is really our oldest home. Here you see its arbors of post oak and willow, the Y-shaped uprights on which the green branches rest, needing neither nails nor binding. These elements simply depend on each other in harmony, as do all the elements of creation.

"Today, during the Busk, we will fast. Tomorrow we feast. Life is filled with such antitheses—dearth and plenty, dark and light, cold and warmth, spirit and body, death and life, old and new. Tonight the old year's fires will be extinguished. All hearths will be swept and spread with clean sand. A new fire will be struck from the flint, which is red with the blood of the sun, then carried to each household."

"There was something about a spiral," Martha said, "symbolic of the earth joined to the sun."

"Yes," said Tsch-kote. "Yonder you see a low mound. It is made of the ashes from all previous square ground fires and is symbolic of the first earth to emerge from primeval waters. On it *Essaugeta Emissee,* the master of breath, stood to complete creation. He commanded Kococúmpu, the evening star, to make light. It was not enough, so he added Huréssē, the moon, and, finally, Hv'se, the sun. He took a small piece of mud and while he was trying to decide what shape man should be, he saw the shadow of his own hand, and so he knew that man should be made in his own image. The spiral pattern of our dances is meant to be seen from above, by *Essaugeta Emissee,* circling, climbing upward toward the sun. The ancient pyramids and ziggurats rise toward the sun, for their makers knew, as we do, that the earth is the womb of the sun, from which springs every living thing."

Tsch-kote took a stick and began sketching on the bare earth beside the table. "Our people have many symbols. From the creation mound, *Essaugeta Emissee* sent forth birds. In the feather dance you will see plumes from the crane, which represent peace, and those of the hawk, representing war. The rainbow is a symbol of the tie between earth and sun, for the sun draws up the vapors which make the rainbow. You see the rainbow represented in the ribbons Johnson wears on his shirt, and in the ribbon dance our ladies will do. Johnson's shirt is a 'hunting shirt,' and does not mean that he is hunting animals, but that he is hunting knowledge."

Martha asked, "Why do you say the square ground is your oldest home?"

"All these symbols were known to the ancient Mesopotamian civilizations," Tsch-kote replied. "You will find a good description of our Green Corn Festival in Leviticus, chapter twenty-three, verses thirty-three to forty-two."

Martha pondered. "It is all so mystical. So thought-provoking. Why do you call it so crudely a 'stomp dance'?"

"That is the white man's term," he said. "This country has drawn to it some rough and vulgar people who rudely denigrate all Indian things in the most crude manner. Indians have been guilty of accepting some of their terms. We are all guilty to some extent."

Resting his stick on the table, Tsch-kote arose. "I must pay my respects to your square ground chief, Heléswv. Then I must visit about the camp during this quiet day of fasting while our people take time to be contemplative. So many of our problems arise from haste, from failing to take time to think things through to the possible implications of hasty acts."

He breathed deeply. "Tomorrow is the ball game. It is the equivalent of, and often the substitute for, war. To the *tustannuggee* it is *rv'hv-en-hórrē*, the 'brother of war,' often used to settle disputes between antagonistic groups. It serves to burn off man's old aggressions, freeing him from enmity to enter the new year in peace of mind. Perhaps," he turned his attention to Johnson, "after the ball game we can discuss the matters that are troubling you."

Johnson acquiesced. One did not try to tell the chief what to do. He watched Tsch-kote climb into his buggy and drive away. At the edge of the square ground he unhitched his horse and led it around, tying it so that it could munch on a portion of the bale of hay he broke open in the rear of the buggy, then disappeared inside the *chokofa*.

Diffidently, Johnson told Martha, "I'm supposed to take part in some things today."

"Yes," she said. "Don't worry. I'll be watching, trying to learn. Perhaps you should lend me your 'hunting shirt.'"

Johnson smiled with growing confidence. "You've already found out more than I ever have wearing it."

He heard Auntie Kerfetu's voice then, speaking out from the quilt enclosure in which she had spent the night. "You had better be wearing it to hunt for some answers to the questions Tsch-kote will be asking you after the ball game," she called out.

The strenuous rituals of the day kept Johnson busy, but Martha Ann was never out of his thoughts, for he frequently found himself looking, and always finding her, sitting with Auntie Kerfetu, sitting alone, but always pensively watching, seeming as wistfully alone in the crowd as he seemed to feel. As the morning became afternoon and the summer locusts set up their clacking, in the rising and falling din of their noise, he seemed to gain strength, as he always did during the Busk.

Past midafternoon, Johnson led the young children in a dance. They spiraled out from the fire to the four corners of the square ground, singing a song in which Johnson gave the cry of the wild goose and the youngsters in response sang, "The little geese sleep . . . gosling, go to sleep with your head beneath your wing . . ." to the sharply accented rhythm of the tortoise shells' rattling.

It was a good thing for the children, Johnson knew, for it taught them to honor the great wild birds who could find their way across vast distances as these children would have to find their ways through the turbulent years of life. It helped them to learn to dance and sing toward the day when they would inherit the responsibility of carrying on these ceremonial ways.

Martha clearly found sheer joy in the chanting and motion of the children, and in Johnson's leading them, for he could see her eyes sparkling in her shining face as she sat bolt upright, entranced. As the children echoed the cry of the wild goose in ending the song, she broke forth in clapping applause like a white audience, to the startled amusement of the Indians observing from the people's arbor. They expressed an equal pleasure in the children's singing and dancing, in excited talking and joyous laughter as proud parents pointed out and commented on their own.

The afternoon was busy as the women were working, cleaning their households, sweeping their hearths and sprinkling them with clean sand, making ready to receive the new fire early in the morning. There would be no sleep for Johnson that night, for he was required to remain in the *chokofa*, observing and participating in the ceremonies with other *tustannuggees*, and taking the *yaupon* medicine drink that would purify him of old-year errors, prepare him to do better in the new year about to begin, and empower him for the ball game tomorrow.

The early evening was filled with the feather dance and, later, social dances, in which the women were permitted to take part. Johnson succeeded in persuading Martha into a few. He would go into the arbor, take both her hands, and try to tug her out into the square ground. At first, her reluctance and embarrassment were nearly impossible to overcome. But after the first time, during which everyone was respectful to her, the warm welcome of the outgoing people won her, and it was not so difficult to persuade her into a procession. Long after the moon had risen he saw Auntie Kerfetu come and lead her away.

He knew they would go to sleep. It was not required that women, children, and the aged stay up all night, though some of them did, and all the *tustannuggees* who would play ball tomorrow had a full night of running dances, strong songs, and purification to prepare them for the ordeal that awaited them come morning. Johnson did not hold back, but gave himself fully, in grave solemnity, to every rite, becoming stronger and stronger as the hours went by.

With the others, he ceremonially handled the burned ashes of the old corn, aided in the ritual of extinguishing the old fire, then went to the river to bathe himself. He returned to the square ground just as the dawn was reddening the eastern sky. Everyone was up and filled with anticipation. It was time to kindle the new fire.

CHAPTER 8

Johnson stood beside the square ground watching the pole boys place the new logs. One pointed to each of the cardinal directions from its place on the clean sand. Heléswv, the square ground chief, then kindled the fire. As the sun rimmed the eastern horizon, he struck the flame.

The small portrait of the sun sprang blazing into new life, and the gathered Creeks moved off toward their own arbors, carrying the fire to their own households. The response of new life seemed to spring up, mounting through every family as their own hearth was relighted, culminating in one great surge that carried them out to the ball ground.

Johnson, stripped to breechclout and moccasins, jogged out toward the playing field among them. He carried in his hands his carefully matched three-foot-long ball sticks, resembling *la crosse* sticks with their end cups of willow strips and rawhide lashings.

Johnson's face and body paint was ash white, in broad inverted V's from his forehead to his heels. His opponents would be painted red. The shapes of a man's paint patterns often came to him in a dream, or were given to him by an older player who had retired from active ball play. As he reached the ball ground, the *hiyákpo-hvtke,* the white team, was rallying at the east end of the two-hundred-yard-long ball field.

The red players were assembled at the opposite end. Between them were gathered a pair of large groups of young girls, chanting in support of favorite players and their favored team. In scanning the players, Johnson concluded there were more than a hundred, split evenly with about fifty on each side. As they came together in the center of the field each player threw down his ball sticks, to be matched by those of an opposing player, to be sure they had the same number on each side.

The cross-hatched goals at the far ends of the field looked tiny and distant to Johnson as he matched his sticks with an opposing player and picked them up again. This year's game would be between the *Tolófuestē*, townsmen who lived in nearby North Fork Town, and the *Tu'lwvestē*, country bumpkins, outlanders gathered from the surrounding clans of the Creek Nation. Johnson was one of the outlanders. His work as a Lighthorseman gave him no regular base he could call home. Buster Vixico was also one of the country bumpkins, for he came from far away, near Eufaula.

Johnson felt no strong antagonisms except, at this particular moment, toward the fact that he had to play at all. He would rather have spent the time with Martha. It had never really occurred to him how little women participated in the Green Corn ceremonies. They were expected to keep their arbors clean, do the cooking, and herd the children, but there were only a few ceremonies in which they could participate. He knew that, in bringing Martha, he had thoughtlessly anticipated idyllic hours with her of the kind he had come to anticipate in the study sessions at the Lewises' cabin. I didn't think it through, he realized. Except for the few dances during the early part of the past evening, in which she had not been especially eager to take part, Martha had had to spend the entire time with Auntie Kerfetu, or alone.

So he wished he could sit beside her now, as a spectator, rather than being obligated to take part. He felt ill at ease in his paint. Although it was white, the color of peace among his people, Martha might not see it so. She might look on it as evidence of some latent savagery.

Johnson trotted past the stake-holders' station, where the wagers of the opposing teams were held. He owned nothing he could spare, was not a gambling man, and had wagered nothing, but around the stake-holders' arbors were tied cattle, horses, dogs. There were heaps of blankets, piles of articles of clothing, stacks of big and small boxes containing tobacco, money, anything, everything one could bet on who might win the game. In days not long gone, a man might bet his wife, or his life, on the outcome of the game. The first team to score nine goals, each tallying one point, would win. There was no time limit. The game might be completed this morning, or might run on into the afternoon, with time out for the spectators, but not the players, to eat.

Each player was under compulsion to keep the busk, his fast, until after the game was over. Johnson knew that the North Forkers had the advantage. Living in close proximity to one another, they had the opportunity to practice ball handling and passing, to devise strategies for the unified surges that could carry a team to the goal. Some of Buster's Crazy Snake partisans were North Forkers, but most were with Buster on the white team.

A brief wonder at the temperate behavior of the Snakes during these past days again touched Johnson. Obviously, the strength of the Green Corn traditions still had the power to bring his Creek people together. Heléswv came strolling onto the field, carrying the game's small deerskin-covered ball, and Johnson jogged over to stand beside Buster Vixico.

"You reckon we can beat these town bucks?" he asked amiably.

The hostile Vixico turned and walked away without a glance, his face obdurate. Johnson shrugged inwardly. Every man was pretty much alone in this game, and Buster probably preferred it that way. The square ground chief tossed up the ball. An agile townsman, outreaching everyone, caught the ball in his stick cups with a shout, and hurled it over everyone toward his opponents' goal. Both teams swept downfield in pursuit of it.

The partisan girls and women on the sidelines screamed and leaped, crying out encouragement or yelling for vengeance. A glance as he ran showed Johnson that people were still making wagers. Considerable lines stretched out from both the stake-holders' places. Three more adroit passes and the deerskin ball hurtled through the uprights of the white goalposts. An easy one, thought Johnson amid the shrieking and cheering. He heard someone call out, *"Hum'ken pvsv'tke!"*—one dead—one goal scored.

He saw one of his teammates, in a vicious swing, strike the goal maker across the back with his ball sticks. The blows were vindictive revenge for the goal maker's success, and the successful townsman turned, lashing in anger at his attacker. There were no rules against roughness in this game. The ball was in play again and a townsman caught it, but Johnson's outlander teammates were incensed at the ease with which the first goal against them had been made. They were surely the stronger team, muscled from work and hunting and not soft-ened by town living. They took possession of the ball by sheer physical force, driving it relentlessly toward the red goal.

Score! Even Johnson felt a lift as his teammates stamped and gobbled, celebrating their first taste of victory with war cries. The ball went up again and the bumpkins scored again. The townsmen began to play with vengeful determination. The ball was driven up and down the field. Players on both sides were thrashed bloody in a torrent of lashing sticks, knee kicks, and elbow hits.

The North Forkers scored the next three goals. Johnson glanced up at the sun. He was astonished that it had risen so high. They had been punishing each other for a long time. He was greasy with sweat, his paint streaked and running. The game had reached a point where it took a hard look to be sure whether the player to whom you moved to pass was red or white. The score changed again, now standing at four white, five red.

He eagerly netted the ball in his stick cups and ran head-long toward the red goal, leaping up high with his arms at full cock. Johnson had extended himself backward to hurl, his eyes

scouring the playing field for a white teammate to pass the ball
to, when he saw the coming red. The opponent came charging
at him like a wild timber hog. It was too late to make any de-
fensive move.

Johnson was hit in midair. A red assailant, his fat belly
hanging over his tight-knotted breechclout, crashed a meaty
shoulder into Johnson's guts. The momentum of their collision
in full flight doubled Johnson over like a deflated bladder. As
he was hurled to the ground like a dead weight, time stopped
for Johnson Lott. Only half sensible, he did not know how far
he had been thrown by the impact, or how long he lay before
conscious thought began to filter into his pain-addled brains.
The *pokkec'etv* ball game forbade the use of guns or knives.
Anything else was legal. The only way to get through it was to
be in hard physical condition, with a belly emptied by previous
fasting and purging. Then maybe you could survive.

Johnson lay stunned, staring up at the sun. The action of
the ball game was proceeding furiously, almost a hundred
yards from where he lay. Painfully, pumping air into his aching lungs, he managed to raise himself on one arm, then sit upright. He was not the only casualty of the game. Downed men
were strewn about the field, some unmoving, others struggling
to rise. Blood trickled from the mouth of a prostrate teammate
near Johnson, though the man's eyes were open and alert. His
body was patchy with dried blood from deep scratches the
medicine man had made in his arms and legs during the game-
preparation ceremonies of the night before.

The gar-tooth scratches sometimes helped to prevent muscle
spasms. Johnson yelled at him, asking the score of the game.
His bleeding teammate held up five fingers and pointed toward
the white goal, then eight fingers, pointing toward the red goal.
Five to eight in favor of the red North Fork Town team. The
game had a ways to go yet.

Johnson struggled to his feet. His white-painted teammate
nearby hawked, spat out a gout of blood, rolled over, and lay
still. Visibly, he had been battered more than enough. He was

out of the game. Johnson, staggering, started across the field toward the action. His senses were reeling and swimming and he was thankful for yesterday's and last night's fasting and purging.

If he had had anything inside him he would be vomiting it now. He was sick from the hair on his head to the soles of his feet. Haltingly, against growing resistance, he tried once more to enter the obstinate currents of the fray. The red team was moving the ball toward the white goal and Johnson saw that one of the downed players on the fringe of the melee was Buster Vixico.

There was no movement of breathing in Vixico's limp heap of flesh. Johnson moved toward him, drawn by the possibility that the Crazy Snake leader might be dead. Men had been killed before in the *pokkec'etv* game. As thudding heartbeats pumped blood and oxygen into his brain, Johnson gained a little more equilibrium. Trying for more speed as he shifted direction and sprinted toward Vixico's body, Johnson saw the same fat red-painted player who had struck him down come hurtling out of the vortex of play action.

As the red player came out of the squirming, struggling mass of players, all straining to control the ball, he was obviously seeking isolation. Hoping to position himself to receive a thrown pass, which he could then propel between the white goalposts and end the game, the red player began circling out.

Then he saw the prostrate body lying beside his path. The temptation to do further violence to a fallen white enemy was plainly too great. He veered from his course. Vaulting upward, the sweat-streaked North Forker hurled himself bulkily into the air with the intention of stomping both feet on Vixico's body.

Johnson's anger flared at the useless, sadistic violence of such a brutal act, and he altered his own course. As the North Forker had attacked him earlier, Johnson launched himself at the middle of Buster's attacker.

The collision seemed as jarring as the previous one, and the stomper was knocked aside before his feet hit the prostrate Vixico, though Johnson did not have enough body weight, and he was too tired, to have any devastating effect on the fat man. The North Forker fell on his pratt, where he sat dizzily for only a moment, then leaped up and ran circling out to receive his pass.

On the ground, Johnson got groggily to his knees and hunkered there. He saw Buster's obsidian eyes swivel to stare up at him, bright with lively hate. Vixico was a long way from dead. Johnson wondered if Buster had not simply chosen to take himself out of the game for a little rest and, after a time, would get up to rejoin the rampaging struggle, in its last throes a chaos of pell-mell scrambling and riotous fighting. He looked up in time to see the red player he had knocked on his tail receive the pass he had run out for and traject it through the white goal.

The ninth point had been won. The game was over. Johnson got up to leave the field and saw Martha running out from the sideline toward him. The surviving red players were strutting and gobbling to celebrate their victory, and Vixico stood up. Johnson confronted him. "Buster, I saved your life," he declared. His challenge was only a gesture of revenge for Buster Vixico's shunning him, for Johnson had no real thought that he had done any such thing. Buster stared at him with dull, unfeeling eyes, the same as always. Johnson looked at the callous stare and, this time, he detoured around Vixico. Martha was almost upon them anyway.

She seemed distraught, seizing his bloody arms to say, "I tried to come to you while you were lying unconscious back there, but Auntie Kerfetu and Rebecca wouldn't let me. They said it would shame you to have a woman running to help you."

Johnson was not so sure. The pain and soreness he felt throughout his flesh, in every bone, seemed to respond to this special woman's touch. He let her lead him, greasy and stinking, to Cu'sē's brush arbor. There she sat him down. She dipped a washcloth into a potion simmering in a black kettle over glowing coals of the new fire.

The cloth steamed as she wrung it out while saying, "Auntie Kerfetu and Rebecca brewed this of sweet gum balsam and arnica root." Gently, carefully, she bathed away the sweat, dirt, grime, and drying blood. He was too exhausted to feel any emotion other than gratitude for the palliative flow of the warm liquid across his arms, chest, back, and the quivering muscles of his legs.

It was fragrant of balsam, redolent of the heady and astringent arnica, from which it had been made. As he relaxed now, out of the driving urgency of the hard-fought *pokkec'etv*, his muscles quivered uncontrollably. As tortured flesh gained relief, he became drowsy. Gratefully, he leaned back against Cu'sē's supper table and let his sleepy gaze drift out beyond the perimeter of the arbors. There, fuzzy and out of focus, he could see the horses, Pos'ketv and Hoktecákv, grazing in the mottled sun and shade of the afternoon.

He thought, When she is finished, I will go out there beside the horses and go to sleep. Marveling drowsily at the healing ministrations of her gentle hands, he recalled Tsch-kote's saying that Martha was an Aramaic name meaning "genteel." Listlessly, he remembered that he had given the mare Hoktecákv that name because it was a Creek word meaning "fine lady." He tried to explain the comparison, and the seeming coincidence of this, to Martha. In his languorous fatigue, his explanation must have been as fuddled as the maunderings of a drunken man, but she finally seemed to understand.

"Oh," she said, "you mean your horse?"

"No," he said. "Your horse. I gave her to you."

She looked at _him_ in puzzlement. "You gave her to me? When?"

"At your house," he said. "Before we started over here to the Green Corn Dance."

"Why, I didn't understand," she admitted. "But Hoktecákv is too valuable to give to me," she fussed. In the middle of her protesting he got up and wandered, somnolent, out to the grove where the horses were grazing.

He lay down. His weary body savored the light breeze blowing across him, his skin still coolly damp from the anointing blend of balsam and arnica. He lay there in the shifting, mutable shade, listening to the buzzing of insects. The sound of the horses, steadily cropping grass, was soothing. He was asleep.

The clangor of an iron spoon beating on a cast-iron kettle awakened him. The shadows blanketing him had shifted across his knees and ankles. They indicated that it was late afternoon. The savory odor of roasting ears drifted out from the square ground, a sure sign that the feast was getting underway. Feeling stiff, but rested, Johnson retrieved his drying cloth and walked down to the river. A short swim where the water eddied against the rocks beneath overhanging willows was refreshing. He dried himself, dressed, and went to hunt for Martha.

She was busy, along with the other women, serving food on the long tables that had been strung together end to end beside the square ground. With the heaping platters of roasting ears that he had smelled as soon as he had awakened were steaming bowls of *sofkee*, open jars of home-canned pawpaws, dishes of pickles, poke greens, broadswords of freshly grated corn tied and cooked in cornshucks, squaw bread, pork and hominy, ham and hominy, ham and beans, roasts of beef and smoke-cooked wild game, fried chicken, comestibles brought by visiting tribesmen, Choctaw *pashofa* and *tom fulla*, Chickasaw plums, Cherokee *connutchee*, pitchers of milk, molasses, and honey, possum grapes, red wild plums, blue dumplings, box elder syrup, and hickory nuts.

The queue of feasters, eager for the banquet, was already lined up, passing alongside the tables, each carrying his own plate, knife, fork, spoon, and a drinking vessel for the crockery vats of cold lemonade, tea, or hot coffee waiting at the end of the appetizing tables. The mingled scents, the very sight of so much food, drove home to Johnson that the busk was over. He had fasted for a night and a day, and now felt like he was starving. Grinning, he made his way up to Martha Ann, interrupting her work.

"Now you see," he accosted her, "why there are so many fat Indians."

"It's an example I need," she said. "I've always been so skinny."

"My team got beat pretty bad," Johnson admitted, "and I'm pretty sore. But I do feel like I can sit up and take nourishment."

"Here," she said, "I'll fill a plate for you."

"One plate isn't going to do it." He took an empty plate from the stack in her hands and went off to the end of the line.

By the time he had waited his turn, working his way up through the line, she had finished her work at the serving tables and was able to join him in serving herself. They found a shady place and sat cross-legged on the leafy ground while they ate. As always before at the Green Corn Festival he was astounded at the sheer physical sensation of eating after the long abstinence from food. Energy seemed to flow outward through him like heat from strong drink.

He spoke of it to her. Martha agreed. "It's like bread dough rising in the yeast pan," she said.

He was surprised that she had fasted, too. As a visitor, it was not required of her.

"No," she said, "after Mr. Tsch-kote's explaining, and you persuading me to dance, I decided that I wanted to enter in, the best I could, and get the feel of everything."

Auntie Kerfetu walked by, and her passage, with Martha's words, reminded him.

"I have to talk with Chief Tsch-kote," Johnson said. "He said after the ball game—"

Auntie stopped. "He has gone on to Coweta," she told him over her shoulder, "while you were sleeping. You are saved from having to tell the truth for a little longer."

Johnson felt no strong disappointment—rather, relief. He was grateful, but it was a guilty relief. Martha was intent on finishing her supper. After the feast had been cleared away, the women—suddenly, it seemed—disappeared. Johnson knew what was coming, and that he had a long wait.

The men idled around the square ground, smoking, resting from the stressful excitements and exercises of the day. An hour crept by. The sun set. In that quiet time of evening when solid objects lose their depth and in an instant turn into flat, black silhouettes, Heléswv came into the center of the square ground. He was small, old, but decisive in movement and quick in action. Johnson had often heard him, in spite of his slight size, utter a war cry that would raise the hair on the nape of your neck and could be heard for two miles. The aged square ground chief moved about briskly, his quick gestures supervising the pole boys in building up the new fire.

The chanters began singing. In the magic twilight of the ending day, the women returned. They came in slowly, dancing in a single line, weaving out from the arbors. Each wore a long dress, with beautifully multicolored ribbons streaming to the ground from the tortoiseshell comb in her hair. Shawls in gay colors covered their shoulders, beneath glistening, dangling, silver, coral, and beaded earrings. Innumerable strands of beads adorned the neck of each dancer. A few wore, beneath their long skirts, terrapin shells which they could move silently until the song of the chanters required the rhythmic chatter of their pebbles. Then the pebbles clattered in accenting the chanters' song.

The line came in to circle the fire. The square ground was full of the bright hues of ribbons and moving skirts, from beneath which peeked shapely sandaled or bare feet. When four full circles had wound themselves around the fire, all became stationary, facing the chanters. The fire blazed up, its flickering light falling gently on pretty faces and blouses, as the wearers of the terrapin shells kept time with the chanters without shifting their position. From the ends of the line, two matronly women broke off to circle around all the rest, carrying notched sticks from which feathers floated.

The encircled dancers resumed their motion, making a spiraled kaleidoscope of interlocking rings. Every eye among them, in humility and modesty, was fixed on the ground. It was the privilege of the old men to pass comments aloud, some of them ribald, and an occasional young girl was forced to stifle a smile or a giggle with her handkerchief, but the young men, the Creek warriors, observed in respectful silence.

So did Johnson. He searched the spiraled files for Martha's face, then found her, sitting behind him. "It is the ribbon dance," he said unnecessarily.

She whispered, "The ladies offered to share their finery with me so I could dance with them, but I just wanted to watch. Isn't it beautiful?"

They were spiraling off the square ground, dancing as gracefully as they had entered it, and returning as soon as they left. The Old Dance songs, which followed, would begin immediately, and all, both men and women, would dance during this final social evening of the Green Corn Festival.

Johnson persuaded Martha out among the dancers with him for a few of the Old Dance songs, but he did not want to keep her away from home for another full night. Soon he went to get Pos'ketv and Hoktecákv. He saddled their two horses and they rode off to return to the Lewis cabin under the bright light of a new moon.

The Lighthorsemen rode through the vast encampment of the Muskogee Indian Fair, getting acquainted with each other's families.

"This is young Lee, who is six," Dewey introduced his son, "and this is my daughter, Susie. She's nine. Both of them are smarter than their papa or their mama."

Dorcas, his wife, was a pretty Chickasaw woman whose face showed the worry lines of trying to raise a young family alone. "Their papa,"—she smiled—"isn't home enough for them to find out how smart he is." She stood before their neatly erected wall tent, keeping an eye on the breakfast fire. Its smoke climbed, thin and faint, toward the wide, sheltering spread of tarpaulin high above them.

The encampment stretched the capacity of the fairgrounds. Dewey's Chickasaw people were near the long crafts exhibit building, neighboring the adjoining Choctaw contingent. The carnival sprawled to the east, where the Ferris wheel was spinning. Its tinny music floated over them, along with the sounds of barkers' voices urging passing sightseers to throw at their rag dolls and win a gewgaw.

Beyond the carnival stretched the Cherokee camp. The Creeks flanked the fairground entrance, near the Seminoles. Visiting delegations of Kickapoo, Iowa, Sac and Fox, Shawnee, Peoria, Miami, Delaware, and Potawatomi ringed the perimeter. Space had been left vacant for the not-yet-arrived Kiowa and Comanche. A few Pawnee and Osage had come, situating themselves on opposite sides of the campground, for their long struggles with each other had made them wary, and the Osage's deep-rooted enmity with the Cherokee made them particularly chary.

Dorcas said, "I know you all don't have time to stop for breakfast, so I'll only offer you a sweet roll to eat while you ride."

Each of the Lighthorsemen accepted the helping of sugar-sprinkled squaw bread she proffered, and rode on to the Choctaw camp where Buck Tom, wiping the sugar off his mouth, delightedly presented them to his "old lady" Ehiwu. The smile on her broad, dark face was missing an upper tooth, but lacked nothing in outgoing warmth and sincerity.

She asked cheerfully, "Is the Reverend behaving himself?"

Millar looked around curiously. "The Reverend?"

Buck Tom grinned, and said, laughing, "We held a protracted meeting down in the woods by Bokhoma while I was home. Now I'm licensed to preach the white man's religion."

"So you'll be working on us," Millar speculated.

"I never saw a bunch that needed religion more," Buck declared.

Dismounting, they enjoyed a helping of *tom fulla* around Mrs. Tom's breakfast fire, then rode on toward the fairground entrance, stopping in the big Seminole camp, where it was Mutt's turn to do the honors.

"This is my wife, Faith," he said, "and these are my three sons, Tvskanvke, Tvskahóma, and Tvskekingē."

Handsome and dignified Faith Kiley waved a teasing arm at her husband. "Mutt ought to be ashamed of himself," she bantered. "They haven't had a white schoolteacher yet who's been able to learn to say their names!"

She fixed them each a sandwich of cured ham in shuckbread.

Munching these savory portions, they rode around the carnival ground to the Cherokee encampment while Millar deviled Mutt about his sons' difficult Seminole names. As they entered the varied assortment of Millar Stone's many-shaped tents, brush arbors, tarps, and even one tepee, Mutt Kiley tried for revenge.

"Great mogul!" Mutt exclaimed. "It looks like a whole tribe, maybe Arabs, has settled in here. Where is the oasis, oh noble nabob?"

Gratifyingly, Millar was flustered. "Well, I've got my wife, all my kids, and five grandkids spread out around here."

"Who does that tepee belong to?" Mutt asked. "I sure never heard of a Five Civilized Tribes Indian living in a tepee before!"

"It's mine," Millar admitted. "I got to looking at them while we was down in the Kiowa country. When I come home this time Mamie 'n me got busy an' made one. It's mighty comfortable. You see there, she's got one side rolled up. In the summertime it's real cool that way. If we go anywhere to camp out this winter, we'll just put a ground cloth in it and we'll be as snug as bugs in a rug. Sue Ellen, our oldest still at home, pretty much takes care of the baby and our two youngest ones now. That gives Mamie 'n me some private time together nowadays."

"So there'll be another baby on the way pretty soon," Mutt predicted.

"No, sir," Millar said firmly, "and you'll see why right quick. Hey, everybody out!" he shouted. "I've got some folks here you'll want to get acquainted with."

Heads began to appear, timidly, between the tent flaps. The youngsters emerged, exhibiting congenial sibling rivalry. There was some pushing and shoving as Millar mustered them into line. Even the adults present cooperated, laughing, talking, a good deal of it in Cherokee, as the amiable Lighthorse captain started, "This is my oldest son, Aaron, his wife Edna, and their three, Millar II, Malinda, and Calvin.

"This is my daughter Blossom, who married a Creek husband." Millar looked around. "Where's Ehē?"

The young matron made some reply in Cherokee.

"Them boys!" Millar despaired. "Her husband is over on the carnival grounds looking for two of my boys. Anyway, these are my granddaughters, Zelda and Naomi.

"My kids at home," Millar went on down the line, "are Sue Ellen. She's nineteen. Like I said, two of the boys, Emmett and Tsa-ya, are over running around the carnival. Then this is my pretty girl Osdahiye, she's fourteen. Then Elvin, little Mamie, Adelva—that's Cherokee for goodness—Sophia, and this is my wife Mamie, and the baby, Amos. But that's all there is going—"

Johnson, listening with one ear to the calling of the Stone family roll, had been watching a man making unsteady progress among the ropes securing the backs of the tents along the carnival midway. The erratic, stumbling man stopped behind the lengthy tent housing the freak show. He pulled a bottle from his pocket and took a long drink. Johnson, during the drink, had nudged his captain in midsentence.

Millar stopped talking and looked. Johnson's chin pointed. By now all five of the Lighthorsemen were watching the staggering Indian. Another tribesman came around the freak tent, stopped, spoke to the drinker, and held out his hand. The drinker shook his head. A short argument ensued. Then the bottle owner began gesturing. The general direction of his unsteady pointing seemed to be toward the fairgrounds entrance, and his inquisitor turned around and started that way.

"Let's see where he's going, gents," Millar suggested. "Fan out, and keep back in the crowd. One of us ought to be able to keep him in sight."

As they converged, afoot, on the upper end of the carnival midway, then on the entrance gate, Johnson did not need to keep the man in sight. There, beyond the fairground's ornate rustic archway, he saw a gnarled little man wearing a blue stocking cap.

The *kawnakausha's* stocking cap covered his bald dome. He wore a knee-length linen duster and stood on the let-down tailgate of a tall boxed wagon—the kind patent medicine peddlers used in traveling about the Indian Territory.

On the wagon's high, broad side a red devil was painted, holding a three-tined pitchfork in one hand and a bottle labeled "Satonic" in the other. From the tailgate platform, Bluejay the medicine man was making his spiel for the curative powers of the elixir he purveyed. The man the Lighthorsemen were following was making a beeline for the patent medicine wagon.

It was a touchy business. Johnson hung back, hardly knowing what to do. The prospective Indian buyer homed in on his target. He spoke upward to Bluejay, cutting off his spiel. Johnson, not wanting to fall too far behind, hurried on toward them through the crowd.

The elfin bootlegger leaned down from the wagon and his hand motions were as dexterous as a prestidigitating sleight-of-hand magician's, but as he attempted to pass a bottle, Bluejay found his wagon surrounded by five grim-faced Lighthorse policemen. His small hand, still holding the pint bottle, disappeared under the duster as rapidly as it had appeared.

"Its healing ways are satanic. Buy a bottle of 'Satonic'!" he sang out, turning to crawl back into his wagon, but Mutt and Dewey had seized his ankles, pulling him down from the tailgate, and Millar Stone flung open the linen duster. Its lining, from armpits to hem, was pocketed, and a bottle protruded from every pocket.

Bluejay turned surly. "I'll sting you redskins like a hornet! For what you do you need a warrant," he threatened. Seeing Johnson, he eyed him vindictively. "I already know the way to make this dirty Indian pay."

"Take it easy, mister," Millar soothed. "Dewey, has he got a gun?"

Lee Dewey lifted a pepperbox from Bluejay's hip pocket. He released Bluejay and ejected six .25-caliber cartridges from the barrels of the little pistol. "Yep," Dewey said blandly, "there's a stinger for each of us, and one left over."

Bluejay's voice changed from vinegar to honey. "Please depart—my demand is urgent. You persecute an innocent merchant." He wizarded a roll of greenbacks from his pocket, peeled off several of the long green bills, and surreptitiously offered them.

Buck Tom leaned, making a feint toward the money, but kept on bending and lifted a pint from inside Bluejay's boot top. He read the label on the bottle. "The man is right, Millar," he declared. "Listen here. Satonic; Healing Ease for Man or Beast. Analgesic, Antiseptic, Stimulant. Cures Dyspepsia, Diphtheria, Dropsy, Epilepsy, Fainting Spells, Gall Stones. My goodness, Millar, we can't interfere with this good man on his mission of mercy!"

Bluejay, convinced that he had won support, insisted triumphantly, "I wasn't on the fairground. I insist upon my right. You don't own the town around, and me you cannot smite!"

"It isn't where you are—it's what you're selling, mister," Captain Stone said doggedly. "Selling whiskey to Indians is illegal, where*ever*."

In piety, Bluejay intoned, "Here's the label. Again, peruse!

It clearly states this is not booze. I have a license to sell my cure, signed by the mayor. I am pure!"

Millar took the bottle Bluejay gave him and handed it to Johnson. "Taste that, Private Lott," he ordered brusquely.

Johnson pulled the cork, sniffed at the dark-brown, sweetish-smelling concoction it contained and knew that, whatever the consequences, he now had to tell the truth. He did not drink it, but handed the bottle back to Millar. "I couldn't say what it is, Captain Stone. But it smells just like what we took off the Crazy Snakes down at Eufaula, and I can take you to the place where it's made. I found this fellow's factory."

Millar studied him. "I've been thinking you knew something, but I knew there wasn't any use pushing you 'til you got ready. Let's go at it like this. There's no use filing any local charge against this gent. You and Buck go on to his factory. You might accidentally spill his medicine there and stumble over his machinery some whilst I take this medico up to Marshal Fletcher Parr's office in Tahlequah. He can transport our medicine man to Fort Smith, where they can analyze his medicine."

Bluejay's glare at Johnson was fetid as he rhymed, "A bard has said the policeman's lot is not a happy one. The troubles of your Martha Ann have only just begun!"

The nooning air was stifling, hot, and still as Johnson and Buck Tom began their ride south from Muskogee. After an hour, there seemed to be no air. They rode in a sweltering, airless pocket of vacuum so still that even the movement of their horses did not stir enough breeze to dry their own sweat.

"Weather breeder," Buck said.

Johnson agreed silently. He was too numbed with worry to make easy talk. How long before Bluejay's betrayal of the Lewises would bring a posse down the Texas Road? With the Lighthorsemen policing the fair, it would be a makeshift posse, a bunch thrown together. It could even be Crazy Snakes. There were plenty of Indians who hated whites.

Johnson had tormenting visions. What if the Lewises resisted. If the posse was bent on removing them too hastily it could get bloody. Silan Lewis, though a reasonable man, might have a breaking point. What if the posse was led by some mean Indian. Buster Vixico was strong on devilment. What if Martha and her dad put up a fight and got killed?

Buck asked, "How long is it going to take us to get to your bootlegger's factory?"

Johnson pulled himself together. "It took me three days before, but I was hunting it. Now I know where it is. We'll be there before dark."

By the time they reached Webbers Falls, past the middle of the afternoon, the storm was dimly visible on the horizon. They crested the successive peaks south of the falls, watching the distant clouds, black and low and roiling with wind though the rough country through which they rode was still hot and sun-swept. Nothing was stirring. Leaves hung lifeless. The peter bird's calls sounded jittery and nervous.

They had covered maybe twenty miles since leaving Muskogee. The Arkansas River was out of sight now. Buck Tom must have sensed Johnson's agony for, when he invaded it, it was to say, "Millar has a lot of confidence in you, boy."

Johnson rose out of his misery to admit, "I appreciate it. Wish I deserved it."

"Millar has sense enough to know who to have confidence in," Buck said.

Johnson knew that he had, in joining the Lighthorse, taken an oath to do what his captain told him to do. Such oaths didn't seem to mean much when you were right up against it. He thought about turning around and heading back to the Lewises'. Here I go, following Pos'ketv's long nose, not doing anything, he thought, because I don't know what to do.

The airless downslope of timber through which they passed became utterly quiet and they could hear the faraway, approaching roll of thunder. The clouds were mounting, piling high and tumbling in the southwest sky, shot through with occasional jagged lightning bolts, followed by the grumbling thunder.

"Whew!" Buck pulled out a wrinkled bandanna handkerchief, took off his hat, and mopped his face. "It'll be a bobtailed bearcat when it gets here."

The stifling air had become so hot that it was hard to breathe.

Buck squinted into the sun. "There's wind in them clouds."

The towering clouds reached up to blot the sun and dark shadows raced over the brilliantly sun-swept hills to their north and east. Wind, seeming suddenly cold after the hot airlessness, sucked in to fill the vacuum. Then came the rain. A spurting sheet of it, driven by the chilly wind, lashed both timber and riders, drenching them.

Buck yelled something, but it was lost in crashing thunder that ripped down through the hills. Lightning tore through the black light that had replaced the sun, shattering a spar of timber a hundred yards from them. Its instant of light was violet and the scent of it was strong in Johnson's nostrils. The rain was pouring on him and he shouted, "What?"

"I said we ought to have sense enough to git in out of the rain," Buck yelled, grinning.

They rode on through the open timber, getting soaked. After the preceding superheat, it seemed bitterly cold. The rain changed to hail, clipping down through tree leaves like grapeshot, bounding off tree trunks and off their own and their horses' backs.

"We going to get a twister out of this?" Johnson called.

"I don't think so. The wind has got too cold."

They rode on through the noisy storm as the hail again turned to rain, the darkness intensified, and the downpour continued. Then the clouds gradually lightened, the thunder and lightning moved off beyond them, and the storm settled down to steady rain, a cold late August rain through which they rode hunched and miserable.

As the sun made an effort to break through, the clouds scattered. The rain let up and quit. Steam rose from their horses' backs, and the sun that had been so oppressive before seemed welcome. Buck pulled off his boots, emptying driblets of water out of them.

"If this leather was to dry on my feet I'd play hob gettin' 'em off," he said.

"Mine are tallowed," Johnson said. "They turn water pretty good. Younger's Bend is off there to our right now." He pointed. "I found Bluejay's still in that high country just this side of where Belle Starr and her owlhoots are supposed to hang out. It will be coming sundown before we get there. You want to stop and build a fire and dry out?"

"Huh-uh." Buck grinned. "Riding in this sunshine will do it quicker. I've got a hunch that rainstorm may be on our side. Let's keep going."

The oppressive heat did not return. In air cleared and freshened, turning pleasantly warm, Johnson took the lead and rode on up into the mountain fastness where he had found Bluejay. The climb was precipitous, an ascent made more difficult this time by the water pouring out of every coulee and draw to gather itself into a raging torrent roaring down what had been a dry gorge when Johnson had climbed up here before.

He heard Buck pull up, and turned to see him mopping his face with the moist wad of his red bandanna. "We're right on the edge of Choctaw country," Buck said. "Another ten-fifteen miles and we'd be in the San Bois Mountains." He adjusted the boots he had hung over the saddle horn by their pull-on straps and settled his sock feet back in the stirrups. They went on.

Their horses were noisy, pawing for footing on the crests and ridges, each hoof making a clopping echo as it struck the slick, wet rocks.

"The still may be guarded," Johnson said.

"More likely that bootlegger will have hired some ignorant Indian to run off a batch for him while he's gone."

Johnson sniffed the air. "I don't smell a doused fire, or any hot mash." He could detect only the sweet scents of freshly rain-washed woods.

Buck asked, "Ain't there no quieter way of getting there?"

"Nope. That's what got me in trouble before. Might as well go as straight to it as the crow flies."

"It would be better if we was crows." Buck reined in and listened carefully. "I don't hear anything but us, and water pouring out of every hollow from here to the Kiamish. Maybe the water noise will hide our racket."

They passed the place where Johnson had left Ceś-sē in the brush, and were there, riding in among the mash barrels and condenser tank with its copper coils winding off through the gushing spring. The still was deserted. Buck stopped beside the collector vat, on which a wooden sign had been hung:

> *Who finds this place and leaves it worse*
> *On him I'll lay a heavy curse! Bluejay*

✓ "In the old days when I was *alikchi* I might have worried about a thing like that." Buck pulled on his boots, got down, and laid his hands against the big copper cooker. "Cool. He must have been afraid to let anyone in on his secret. Except you." Buck grinned.

"I wish I'd never got in on it," Johnson said.

Buck put a boot against the side of the cooker and braced himself against the limestone ledge. "I sure wouldn't want to be accused of malicious mischief if the court should decide that moonshine is patent medicine." He shoved, hard. The cooker rolled off its rock foundation. Tumbling through wet gray ashes where the fire had been cleaned out beneath it, it rolled down the gorge and into the torrent of water racing out of the high country.

Johnson dismounted to overturn a mash barrel, watching its contents spill and mix with the racing white water. Buck pushed the collector vat in behind it. Both of them bent their backs to heave out the copper coils and hurl them into the maelstrom in the rocky hollow.

Buck surveyed the damage. "That big wind a while ago has blowed the whole shebang off its foundations and the rainstorm washed it right down the crick," he lamented. "These late summer thunderstorms do take a toll in loss of property."

He remounted and pulled off his boots. "Let's head on back. It's getting pretty late, but we can make it part ways, camp tonight by Webbers Falls, and go on back to Muskogee in the morning."

Near midnight, sitting in the flickering light of their campfire beside the falls, Buck said, "Bluejay! Don't that bootlegger have no other name?"

"He claims he gave his name away." Johnson shrugged.

"And calls himself Bluejay. The Martha Ann he mentioned. Who's she?"

Like the caving banks of the full-running Arkansas River, Johnson's eroded reserve gave way. As flood waters overflow sandy land, he told Buck about the Lewises, about Martha's teaching him, and how worried he was about the consequences of Bluejay's telling all this to the authorities.

Buck evinced no great concern. "Why, boy, that bootlegger has got nobody to preach to but Fletch Parr and that bunch over at Fort Smith. They don't care a lick how many whites settle on Indian land. Bluejay's tattle may never find its way back to the Agency, which is the only place anybody would be apt to do anything about it. I sure wouldn't worry until somebody starts something."

"But he'll tell Millar—and Mutt—and Dewey!" Johnson protested.

"He'll be talking to your friends," Buck said noncommittally.

CHAPTER 9

As they approached the arch of the fair's rustic gateway and passed the place where Bluejay had been caught, all Johnson's fears bestirred themselves. Heavy foot traffic slowed their horses to a walk and Johnson saw Millar and his son-in-law, Ehē, standing together beside the carrousel. He reined that way and Buck came along.

The merry-go-round was trumpeting out a squeaky dirge and as they dismounted, Millar, glancing sideways, saw them.

He grinned crookedly. "You fellers want a ride? I'm buying."

"We just finish the better part of a three-days' ride you sent us on to Younger's Bend," Buck chuckled, "and you offer us the big fun of getting off a real horse and onto a wooden one."

"My kids think it's big fun," Millar said. "There's four of 'em on there, and one of Ehē's."

Buck patted the neck of his sweaty, hipshot, tired horse. "We left a crick bed full of busted mash barrel slats and a coil of copper tubing that looks like a acordeen," he reported, "scattered down three-four miles of mountainside with a condenser and a cooker full of dents and holes."

Millar nodded. "We left Johnson's buddy, Bluejay, in Tahlequah with a charge of whiskey-selling to Indians laid against him. He may shake loose from it, but it will take him a while."

He said nothing more. Johnson remembered Buck's advice and thought, As long as the dog sleeps, let it.

"Private Lott." Millar was addressing him. Johnson's stomach felt suddenly hollow. "How about letting my boy Elvin ride your Pos'ketv in the horse race tomorrow? He wants to. Buck, how about you? You a betting man?"

Johnson took a deep breath of passing relief.

Buck said, "Used to be. I'm preaching now."

"Well, you don't have to bet," Millar said. "Me 'n Mutt 'n Lee are letting three of my kids ride those Chickasaw horses of ours."

"Which one would ride my horse?" Buck asked.

"My fourteen-year-old girl, Osdahiye. She rides as good as any boy."

Buck approved. "It sounds like a good match-up."

The trumpeting merry-go-round squealed to the end of an unmusical "Columbia, Gem of the Ocean." Millar's youngsters came trooping in from around its circumference. Elvin was small for his twelve years. His round brown face looked up at Johnson. "Mr. Lott," he appealed, "did my daddy ask you? Can I ride your horse tomorrow afternoon?"

Johnson reached to tousle his hair. "You bet, partner. And I'm going to lay a big bet right on your nose. You bring him in a winner."

"Ehē," Millar asked his son-in-law, "would you take the kids back over to camp? We've got a chore to do."

Johnson and Ehē exchanged a short conversation in Muscogee as Millar's son-in-law gathered the four youngsters together and shepherded them off.

"What was that Creek gibberish about?" Millar asked.

Buck Tom laughed. "Johnson asked him if he had a name."

"Sure he does," Millar declared. "Ehē."

"That only means 'husband' in Muscogee," Buck explained.

Johnson said, "Your son-in-law says his name is Hērēmahē, which means 'important.' Your daughter thought it might make him uppity if she called him that all the time. So she just calls him 'husband.'"

"Well, I'll be doggoned," Millar said. "Here I thought Ehē was the only name he had."

"These women, especially our wives and daughters, are bound to keep us in our place," Buck chortled.

"Well, our place right now is scattered out," Millar said seriously. "These fairgrounds are full of Crazy Snakes, looking almighty militant. Mutt is over in the crafts building keeping an eye on them. Dewey is circulating from one tribal camp to another. I'd been wandering around the carnival 'til E—uh, my son-in-law—brought the kids over. Why don't you two split up among the camps with Dewey? We're going to have to stick tight—"

The jingling of horse bells cut through the carnival noise of the wheezing merry-go-round and haranguing show barkers. The procession of Plains Kiowa and Comanche, in full panoply of feathers, warbonnets, feathered lances, and drawn travois, was slowly entering the fairgrounds. They had painted themselves for the occasion. It was a solemn and barbaric display of power, stern-faced warriors, prancing horses, chiefs, dignified women, all mounted on their finest, most of the young boys leading two or three spare horses as they came in procession through the entrance gate of the fairgrounds.

No Plains warrior looked aside. Each rode proudly tall, his brightly feathered war lance pointed skyward and resting in a stirrup, his stern visage uplifted. The children and a few of the women looked around in curious awe at the jangling confusion of the carnival, at the vast tribal encampments spread farther than their eyes could see, at the long, turreted structures of the exhibit buildings, horse barns, and stables, and the spread-out bleachers of the grandstand.

One of the Kiowas began to sing—a greeting song, Johnson guessed, as he looked and saw that it was Badger. Millar, Buck, and Johnson stood watching the grand entry until it was parallel with them, then Millar said, "Let's go and guide them out to their camping areas, see that they get settled in. We need to find that feller Adam's Apple—there he is, I see him now. Let him know that the big parade through Muskogee is tomorrow morning. We'll end up out on Agency Hill tomorrow noon. Nathan Able has built a fancy new pavilion out there for the peace talks. He's fixing up a big feast to eat after the parade."

Although Johnson had never had time to find the trader Nak-wígv to refresh his memory of the sign language, increasingly what he had once known came back to him during the afternoon and evening. He had plenty of practice, helping Kiowa and Comanche select campsites, guiding groups of Plains Indian women to the fairgrounds well where they could draw water, to the brushy tangles along Bird Creek where they could pull down firewood, keeping an eye on the curious groups from other tribes, some of them Crazy Snakes, who came sneaking around the Plains encampment, furtively watching it.

Johnson kept wishing he could sneak away for a visit to the Lewis homestead, just to see Martha Ann, to see if she was all right. But he did not, and he was busy before sunup the next morning, answering Plains people's questions about the parade, helping Kiowa and Comanche warriors rig and tie their jingling horse bells, secure their accoutrements, and find their places in the parade lineup.

As the whole procession moved off toward town, the five Lighthorsemen met briefly at the fairgrounds gate.

"The main thing," Millar said, "is to keep within signaling distance. Them Crazy Snake wild men might pick the middle of Muskogee to show off. They might take a captive, or kill somebody, or start a shooting war to show how determined they are to prevent allotment."

Mutt was carrying, in the crook of his arm, the double-barreled sawed-off shotgun the West United Telegraph troubleshooter had abandoned to him early that spring.

Millar suggested, "Don't shoot off that cannon, Mutt, unless you have to. You might hurt somebody in the crowd."

"I've never got around to buying any shells for it," Mutt reported casually. "It's still unloaded."

"All right. Let's string ourselves out along the parade route, but keep each other in sight. If anything breaks loose, wave for help and everybody come running."

They mounted up and rode out. The street was lined with spectators, mostly Five Tribes Indians from the fairgrounds encampments, but there were groups of alien whites gathered under the wooden awnings of the raw frame stores built since the opening of the railroad and Johnson heard interesting comments.

A querulous white woman complained, "I do not think such heathen spectacles should be permitted. It gives them exaggerated ideas of their importance. They might run amuck. We could be murdered in our beds tonight."

The merchant standing beside her commented, "This is still the Indian Territory. We're here by their sufferance. If they revoke my permit, I'm out of business tomorrow. Alleviation can come only through allotment. Then we can join together, form a single-minded government, and have a federally appointed white territorial governor."

Neither speaker made any attempt to speak softly or prevent Johnson from hearing. They probably figure I don't speak English, he thought. He rode past Martin & Smith—Boots & Shoes; Perry's Hardware—Farm Machinery; Ransome Reed—Real Estate; The Boudreau House—Lodging; Swinton & Sons—Gen'l Merchandise, Fancy Groceries. Here he paused to watch the parade. He could see Mutt in the distance to his right, and Buck yonder behind him.

The Kiowa had brought a few guests from the Tewa pueblos far to the west, and from among the Crow yet farther to the northwest. Osage, Oto, Sac, and Fox, in roaches and straight-dance costumes, passed him. One elderly Cherokee had dressed as Sequoyah, whose burial place in the Wichitas Millar Stone was sure they had found. He wore a long, striped jacket, leather leggings, and a vermilion turban. In his hand he carried a long willow wand, symbolic of the Cherokee syllabary that Sequoyah had often drawn in the dust at his feet.

Pretty girls in fringed buckskin or colorful beribboned tribal dresses paraded past, mounted on paint ponies.

As the end of the parade neared, Johnson touched Pos'ketv with his spurs and rode alongside the column, past the livery stables and wagon yards interspaced at the edge of town and climbed up on Agency Hill for his first look at Nathan Able's peace-talk pavilion. It was a handsome white building, walled with arches open to the air and large enough to accommodate the conferees themselves. Interested spectators would have to gather around the broad arches, in the shade of the burr oaks and maple trees flanking the pavilion.

Able himself, with the Creek chief and judge Tsch-kote, as well as other dignitaries from the Cherokee, Choctaw, Chickasaw, and Seminole, were lined up in front of the pavilion to greet all who came. Johnson tied Pos'ketv to an oak tree and walked to the pavilion steps to shake hands ceremonially with each of them.

As he passed Nathan Able, the agent said, "No trouble this morning with the Snake faction?" His voice rose in a question already tinged with relief.

"No, sir," Johnson confirmed.

Able shook his head doubtfully. "It would seem to me that they are certain to make some gesture demonstrating their convictions before the fair ends tomorrow."

As the parade terminated on the hill, its participants were lining up before the pavilion where the food was being served. Johnson ate and rode back to the fairgrounds to turn his horse over to Captain Stone's boy Elvin.

"I'll be riding him in the fourth race, Mr. Johnson," the black-haired Indian boy told him.

Johnson wandered on up into the grandstand bleachers to watch and wait.

Mutt and Dewey's Chickasaw horses ran in the first race, but neither won. The race was won by a Comanche horse ridden by an ancient Indian, so old that Johnson doubted he could stay on the horse's bare back until the starting gun of the race. When it was fired the old Comanche rode like a demon, outdistancing everyone and winning going away. Johnson watched Millar's boys Tsa-ya and Emmett riding back toward the paddock slumped in dismay.

He felt thirsty, so he descended from his seat in the bleachers and went around behind the grandstand where he had seen a lemonade stand set up. The woman who came to serve him was Auntie Kerfetu. She stirred the crock of pink lemonade with a wooden ladle, took her dipper, and fetched him out a glass.

"I hear," she said, "that you finally got up your courage to tell what you knew about Bluejay."

Johnson drank off a swallow of the tart, thirst-quenching lemonade and asked, "How did you know about him?"

"I told you," she said.

He nodded. "The blue jay birds who come to eat the scraps you throw out in Nathan Able's backyard told you."

Her smile was abstruse. "There is not much that goes on in the Creek Nation that those birds do not tell me about."

"You knew about Martha Ann before I brought her to you," he said.

Auntie shrugged. "Her neighbors speak well of her."

"And of the fact that I visited there, what do they say?"

She scrutinized him, sharp-eyed. "They say she has taught you some things."

"I can read a little now. I can make the letters, but I have not yet learned to put them together into words very good."

"Keep going," Auntie advised. "She may turn you into an intelligent Indian with some sense."

She left him to serve another customer and Johnson turned his back, leaning against the lemonade counter, drinking another draft of the cool liquid from the tall glass. He watched the steady passing of the crowd coming and going, walking along behind the stands between the crafts building and the carnival midway. He saw Buster Vixico coming toward him, alone as usual.

He is by himself more than I am, Johnson thought. It was nearly time for the next race. Johnson could hear the starter shouting to the race riders. "On the mark now! Get set!" Buster turned to walk under the grandstand bleachers. Instantly, Buster's purpose, like a thrown rope, unreeled itself in Johnson's mind.

He could see Nathan Able, sitting beside his wife, on the boards of the open bleachers. Her hair was pulled tautly back in a neatly woven bun, and as her husband turned to say something to her, Johnson saw Buster's hand pull a derringer pistol from beneath his shirt front. The Creek Lighthorseman knew that the race starter would be lifting his pistol skyward to fire the starting shot for the second race. Buster lifted his arm, pointing the derringer at Nathan Able's face.

It will sound like shot and echo or, if Buster is lucky, like a single shot, Johnson thought.

Able would fall, and only those around him would see him fall. Time would pass before many realized what had happened. Buster's artfully contrived plan would give him time to reach whatever refuge he had planned, or the horse he had waiting somewhere, or maybe he would just disappear in the carnival crowd. Johnson threw the remaining lemonade in his glass toward Buster under the stands.

The cool liquid struck the side of Vixico's face, distracting him, and the race-starting gun went off. As horses' hoofs went thundering down the track in front of the grandstand, Johnson started toward Vixico, whose derringer swung to point at him instead of at Nathan Able. The Lighthorseman knew he could not draw his own holstered pistol, for at the first such threatening move Buster would kill him. He lifted his hands aside, holding them wide apart and far away from his own weapon, but kept on walking.

Ducking low to avoid the lowering bleacher seats and the feet and legs above his head, Johnson advanced to say calmly, "Buster, I'm going to have to arrest you." The gun pointed at him, now gripped in both of Vixico's hands, held steady.

"That would mean the whipping tree," Buster said dully.

"Or an attempted murder charge at Fort Smith," Johnson agreed. "But I've got to arrest you."

"If it's a whipping, you'd have to whip me," Vixico said without emotion.

"I'd hate that, too." Johnson watched Buster's eyes, seeing nothing of sentiment or feeling in them.

A twitch of the gunpoint impelled him and Johnson flung himself aside as Buster triggered the derringer. The short-barreled gun was inaccurate even at this short range and Johnson's sidewise jerk helped, but the bullet caught him, plowing through the flesh of his left ribs, glancing from bone to lodge itself in the heavy, roughhewn bleacher stanchion. Johnson reached and grabbed, managing to seize Vixico about the legs, and they both went down.

Floundering in the dirt, Buster tried to bring the ugly little pistol's second barrel to bear, and Johnson was struggling to hang onto Vixico's jerking, threshing legs when help came. It was Mutt and sturdy old Buck Tom. They came swinging down under the bleachers. A carefully aimed kick by Mutt's frayed moccasin jarred the gun loose and it went skittering across the dusty ground.

Buck threw a headlock around Vixico's neck. As Buck and Johnson dragged the squirming Crazy Snake out into the open, Mutt caught a handful of his hair and his belt buckle and jerked him upright.

Mutt said, "Tsch-kote is sitting up there, not far from Nathan Able."

"I'll go get him and bring him down here," Buck offered genially. "This here assailant is a Creek and so is the Lighthorseman he shot, and we're in the Creek Nation. I reckon that qualifies Tsch-kote to preside. Johnson, poke your horse pistol in this Crazy Snake's belly and help Mutt keep him calm."

Tsch-kote held impromptu court in the lemonade stand, using his bare knuckles for a gavel. Vixico sullenly accused

Able. "You are a white man who is working for allotment."

"That is not the matter at issue here," Tsch-kote ruled. "*You* are accused of shooting a Creek Lighthorse policeman."

Nathan Able spoke up. "May I answer Buster Vixico's charge anyway, Your Honor? I've done my best to prevent whites from settling on Indian land and from setting up illegal enterprises in our Indian towns. In spite of all I can do, a few slip through. I am strongly opposed to allotment. I think, though, it is going to come anyway."

Johnson, listening to the agent's statement, thought of the illegally settled white family he was concealing and felt an uncertainty in his conscience as acute as the pain in his side.

Tsch-kote said to Vixico, "Son, if they arraign you for trying to kill our white agent, it will have to be in Judge Parker's court in Fort Smith, and they'll put you in that godawful white man's prison. You'll come out worse than you went in. This shooting of a Lighthorseman is an Indian affair, however. I think we had better keep it that way. I'd advise you to plead to the charge I've offered you. Are you guilty or not guilty?"

Vixico stood sullenly, refusing to answer, then said coldly, "Guilty."

"Obviously!" Tsch-kote declared with a glance at Johnson's bloody shirt. "I'll have to sentence you to fifty lashes, Buster, and normally we'd administer them right now, but I hate to mar the closing days of this fair. Go on home," he ordered the prisoner. "Come back and report to the Agency next Sunday afternoon. That's day after tomorrow. The arresting officer will then administer your punishment."

Buck took Johnson to his fairgrounds camp, where his "old lady" boiled crushed anemone roots and Buck washed the furrowed wound with the medicine while his wife pounded dried yarrow in the hollow of her primitive log mortar-and-pestle.

"It's a good thing I still carry my sack of herbs," Buck said pleasantly. "If I was still *alikchi*," he joked, "I'd doctor you with a lot more hocus-pocus than this. The medicine works just the same without the hocus-pocus." He dusted the wound with the pulverized yarrow powder. "Now you leave your shirt off and go in our tent and lay down. Go to sleep if you can. This will start healing pretty quick, and by morning we ought to put a cloth over it to keep your shirttail from rubbing it sore again."

In the morning, Millar Stone's boy Elvin came leading Pos'ketv. "He won, Mr. Lott." He looked proudly at Johnson through his wind-tousled dark hair.

Buck told the boy, "No, you won. The horse carried you, but it only did what you told it to. You done it just right, laying back like you did and waiting 'til you were almost at the finish line to run around those other horses."

Mrs. Tom was applying a thin cloth dressing over Johnson's now cool and uninflamed wound. She gave Johnson a fruit jar of boiled anemone and a bag of yarrow powder. "If your ribs start to get sore and red, use this just like we did yesterday evening," she told him.

Buck asked, "How you feel?"

"All right," Johnson said.

"Then Millar wants you to ride up the hill and look in on the peace talking. Best we can find out, the Snakes don't feel so venomous with their head man gone home to anticipate the disgrace of a whipping. A good many of his bunch are breaking camp and going home. Millar thinks we're shut of 'em for now."

Johnson rode unhurriedly through Muskogee streets busy with Saturday traders, arriving on Agency Hill while the peace talk was in session. As he approached the white pavilion he could see through its white arches that the Kiowa leader Charging Bear was making a speech. Kiowa, Comanche, and Five Civilized Tribes Indians filled the pavilion and sat in groups on the shady grass outside. Johnson hung a leg over his saddle horn and stayed in the saddle, listening.

"Eating bear meat is forbidden among the Kiowa," Adam's Apple translated. Charging Bear went on, "When the skin is taken off a dead bear, it looks too much like the body of a man. Sometimes even thinking about a bear can be dangerous. Those of us who have that medicine animal's name have to do special things to wear that name in safety. One time we went hunting with the Comanche and they killed a bear. We had been fighting the Comanche for a long time and a thing like that could have started the war up again. But we did not let it. Comanche can eat bears, but Kiowa cannot. You Cherokee are different from us and so are the rest of your tribes. They have lived around the white man too long. If we are going to be friends we will have to put up with that. We will have to put up with each other and not try to change each other. We have been friends with the Comanche for a long time now, and we will try to be friends with you."

He sat down.

Things were proceeding conspicuously well here. Johnson felt restless. He uncocked the leg he had hung over the saddle horn, threaded his way through the seated groups of listeners, and rode down the hill. Fretfully, yet not knowing what to do about his concern, he walked Pos'ketv slowly back toward town.

In a wagon yard, there on the outskirts of Muskogee, he recognized the Lewises' spring wagon, one high side removed so that Silan's mules, tied beside it, could munch on the forage in the wagon bed. Alongside the mule team was Martha Ann's mare Hoktecákv. They were in town, somewhere, doing their Saturday trading.

The relief he felt was not great, for since his deep worrying at Younger's Bend, he had calmed down enough to reason that if anything serious had happened to a settler family that close to Muskogee, some word of it would have drifted into town. Auntie Kerfetu would have known and hastened to tell him. But that did not moderate his uncertainty and fears about the future. It seemed impossible to Johnson that Bluejay would not stir up some kind of a stink, yet he clung determinedly to Buck Tom's advice—"Don't do anything 'til somebody starts something."

Johnson reined up and turned into the wagon yard. Not much use hunting for them in town. He could miss them somewhere. They could come back here, load up, and be gone while he was prowling through stores along the street. Better to hunker down and wait here, however long it took. He tied Pos'ketv alongside Hoktecákv and sat on his boot heels in the shade of the two horses.

Procrastination is, for some, a hard game to play, and Johnson was sure tired of it. The wisdom of doing nothing until you knew what to do, though sensible, wore thin. He squatted there, glumly doleful. The temptation to throw a buggy wrench into the works was potent. Maybe the resulting mix-up would be something he could deal with. Maybe it would wipe out everything.

His basic patience won out. He could at least talk it over with Martha. Maybe, between them, they could figure out something. The sun moved slowly around his high cheekbone to his forehead. Johnson sat stoically, letting it burn his darkly browned face while he waited and thought.

There was no use in stirring up her father. Silan Lewis would immediately carry out the intention he had long ago expressed—that of going to talk with Tsch-kote, or Nathan Able, which would end it. The law was the law, and they were illegally settled on Creek land. His wait stretched out. The sun crept along overhead, moving the horses' shadows fully away from him. Its direct rays, hot as a branding iron, had begun to scorch his right ear when he heard the tattoo of running feet coming across the hardpan of the baked wagon yard corral.

Johnson stood up because he could no longer sit still and she ran right up to him. He stood looking down at her, somehow expecting her to look hurt, or half angry, but she only looked mischievous and glad.

"I've been wondering," she said. "It seems so long since you brought me home from the square ground—and you haven't been back."

"We had to get ready for the fair," Johnson apologized lamely.

Silan Lewis seemed a bit shocked at her forwardness. "My goodness, Martha," he said. "Don't be bold." He led his mules around to the wagon tongue and leaned, hooking their harness into the singletrees.

Martha Ann untied Hoktecákv. "We didn't really need to bring her." She appeared abashed. "I couldn't resist riding her. She is so gentle. So ladylike."

Johnson pulled her sidesaddle's cinch tight.

"Would you folks like to see the fair?" he asked, hoping for some way to gain time.

"I'd like to," Silan frowned, "but I have to go and load the groceries, then go over by the mill to get the meal." He looked up at the sun. "By the time I've picked up the salt for the live-stock—no, there just isn't time. The chores have to be done before dark."

"Then probably—" Johnson meant to say "probably I might as well tell you straight out, and finally get this over with, but his "probably" prompted a surprising response.

"Martha could probably stay," Lewis mused. "Could you see her safely home this evening?"

Johnson's elation was lost in his confusion. "Sure! I—" He hurriedly gave her a lift up into the sidesaddle and she sat looking down at him expectantly. It produced a joy in him no dread of the future could suppress. He yanked Pos'ketv's cinch up tight, too tight, and as he bent to ease it Silan Lewis gee-upped his mules and drove out of the wagon yard.

Johnson stepped across his saddle in a euphoria fa-miliar to him. Immersed in themselves, they rode through Muskogee, estranged from the mundane world, and tied up outside the crafts building. Martha enjoyed its decorated booths of silver, quilled Crow breastplates, medallions, Tewa glazed pottery, wood carvings, Cherokee weaving, Indian dolls, and basketry. Johnson was once embarrassed to mortification to catch himself walking along holding hands with her, like affectionate children.

They ate their way from the crafts building to the carnival midway, sampling cookery well known to Martha from the Green Corn feast, and carried on a lively conversation with Auntie Kerfetu at the lemonade stand. She entertained Martha with her humor-spiced account of Johnson's capture of Buster Vixico. Even Johnson was surprised when he emerged a hero in Auntie's version, for saving Nathan Able's life.

Auntie Kerfetu ended, eyeing Johnson directly, "This is better than the Green Corn Dance, because you can carry out your policeman duties of patrolling the fair with Martha Ann right beside you."

He saw Indian hands lifting to cover Indian smiles all around them, and felt as embarrassed as when he had caught himself holding hands with her.

They surfeited themselves on candy apples and spun sugar sold by the vendors along the carnival midway, then Johnson found them a place in the grandstand for the afternoon show. It was crowded and she had to sit close to him during the long pageantry of the fair's closing exhibition. The dazzling displays of horsemanship, the intricate Plains dancing, the soaring Kiowa songs, lonely as the windswept country in which the Kiowa and Comanche lived, were delightful to her, though Johnson grew more morose as the afternoon lengthened. He knew that he had, through his own awkward self-consciousness, missed the opportunity for a frank and open discussion with her that had seemed so fortuitously available to him at noon.

In silence, dismayed at finding himself again tongue-tied, he undertook the ride down the Texas Road with her in gathering darkness, escorting her home. Tentatively, she tried to probe his moroseness, but found it an iron facade. He was busy condemning himself.

When they off-saddled by starlight at the little settler house and went inside, they found Martha's father reading, by lamplight, a pile of old newspapers he had gotten in town during the morning's trading. Martha was of a mind to get down the schoolbooks, but Johnson persuaded her to sit down.

Facing them, he forced himself to begin. "You remember that paper you found? The one that Martha put together like pieces of a puzzle—" Something, faint and indistinguishable, touched his nostrils. He went to the door, opened it, and stood, breathing and tasting it with slow inhalation.

"What is it?" Martha asked.

"I guess it is that us Indians still have a better use of our noses than—" He heard the distant horses then, a sound too dim and far away for Martha's or Silan's untuned ears to hear.

A posse was coming. It was better to be overcautious than otherwise. "Maybe you'd better get your gun, Mr. Lewis," Johnson suggested. "You take the window back there by the fireplace. I'll bar this front door, and—" He drew his pistol, but as the horses came nearer, he slid it back into its holster. There were four horses coming, and he had ridden too far with those horses not to be familiar with every possible variety of sound their hoofs could make.

Instead of barring the door, he flung it open and went outside to welcome Millar, Mutt, Buck, and Dewey. They responded with warm friendliness and gentility to his introductions.

"Buck told us about this young lady on the way out," Millar said. "We've been trying, but not too hard, to catch up with you ever since you left town. Nathan Able got a telegram this afternoon, over that wire we tried to cut down. Judge Parker wired him that, according to that little bootlegger we caught, we've got a squatter sitting here on Creek land. Nathan didn't have no choice. I sure am sorry."

"I think Dad and I know what Johnson has been trying to say . . ." Martha admitted.

". . . Ever since Martha put together her jigsaw puzzle," Silan Lewis added, "but it has seemed certain to me that this country is going to be opened. Settlers will be coming in, and we would be no worse than the others. It has been our own choice to wait here, quietly."

"If we cannot wait any longer, we will simply have to go." Martha's voice was subdued. "But before we go, there is something I want to do." She turned to face Johnson squarely, telling him frankly, "You are simply too bashful ever to do it. Johnson Lott," she asked, "would you marry me?"

Buck Tom whooped. "That's why there ain't many buck women. The girl has to do the asking. If she can't get up her nerve—"

Johnson interrupted firmly, "No."

Buck stopped, shaken. "You mean you won't marry this girl?"

There was a good deal of awkward shuffling of feet.

"No," Johnson repeated. "That isn't the way to do it. It's got to be done like this." With an effort, he reached out to take her hand. "Would you be willing to be my wife? I'm only a Lighthorse policeman and on the road a good deal. Your father would have to be here to take care of you while I'm on the scout."

"Well," Millar said, "if you two are going to get married there ain't nothing for us to do. There ain't no law against a Creek warrior getting married and setting up housekeeping."

Buck, standing in the slant of yellow lamplight that shone out through the open door, reached into his saddlebag and brought out the Book. "We can perform the ceremony right now," he said. "I'm licensed."

Hesitantly, Silan Lewis said, "But they're not. A marriage license—"

"Usually comes after the fact in this country." Buck nodded firmly. "We used to say, 'I now pronounce you man and wife.' Now we add on, 'Don't forget to go by and pick up a license the first time you're in town.'"

By the time Buck had finished the ceremony, Silan Lewis had coffee boiling, and Millar was urging, "It's getting late.

Johnson, we can get along without you tonight, but you've got to carry out Tsch-kote's sentence tomorrow."

Johnson muttered, "I'd rather take that whipping than have to give it."

"You'll spend your life," Millar rationalized, "doing things you don't want to do."

Silan Lewis said, "Martha, would you mind if I rode Hoktecákv into town with these gentlemen? My presence here tonight can be dispensed with."

Millar nodded. "You can spend the night at Nathan Able's. The rest of us have the fairgrounds to police while the campers move out, even if we are shorthanded." He winked broadly.

As the Lighthorsemen and Silan Lewis mounted up, Johnson stepped into the doorway with Martha Ann. His arm was around her and he grinned bashfully. "Like Millar says," he acceded, "we all have to do things we don't want to do."

Mr. Burchardt is a native Oklahoman and the author of numerous Western novels. He is a past president of the Western Writers of America, is a retired Naval Reserve officer, and was for twenty-three years the editor-in-chief of *Oklahoma Today* magazine. He has received the Western Heritage Award presented by the National Cowboy Hall of Fame, as well as the University of Oklahoma Professional Writing Award, and has twice won the Tepee Award of the Oklahoma Writers' Federation for the Best Novel of the Year by an Oklahoman.